GIRL, ^NEARLY 16
ABSOLUTE TORTURE

Also by Sue Limb

Girl, 15, Charming but Insane
Girl, Going on 17: Pants on Fire

GIRL, NEARLY 16
ABSOLUTE TORTURE

Sue Limb

DELACORTE PRESS

Published by Delacorte Press
an imprint of Random House Children's Books
a division of Random House, Inc.
New York

www.randomhouse.com/teens
www.charmingbutinsane.com

Educators and librarians, for a variety of teaching tools, visit us at
www.randomhouse.com/teachers

The Library of Congress has cataloged the hardcover edition as follows:
Limb, Sue.
Girl, (nearly) 16, absolute torture / Sue Limb.
p. cm.
Sequel to: Girl, 15, charming but insane.
Summary: Jess knows her summer plans are ruined, but little could she imagine
the huge surprise that awaits her when she visits her dad's home for the first
time in years.
ISBN-10: 0-385-73216-3 (trade) — ISBN-10: 0-385-90245-X (glb)
ISBN-13: 978-0-385-73216-1 (trade) — ISBN-13: 978-0-385-90245-8 (glb)
[1. Dating (Social customs)—Fiction. 2. Friendship—Fiction.
3. Summers—Fiction. 4. Fathers—Fiction. 5. Gays—Fiction. 6. England—Fiction.
7. Humorous stories.] I. Title: Girl, nearly sixteen, absolute
torture. II. Title.
PZ7.L6344Gj 2005
[Fic]—dc22
2004026421

ISBN-10: 0-385-73217-1 (trade pbk.)
ISBN-13: 978-0-385-73217-8 (trade pbk.)

Printed in the United States of America

10 9 8 7 6 5 4 3 2 1
First Readers Circle Edition

FOR NANCY NAPPER CANTER

*D*isaster! Jess tried to hide her horror. Her mum frowned. "What's wrong, sweetheart? It's what you've always wanted. A trip to see your dad! I rang him about it last night and he can't wait to see you! And there'll be sun, sea, art, and ice cream! Plus lots of interesting places on the way down there. It's the holiday of a lifetime. For goodness' sake, Jess! What's the matter?"

Jess could not possibly, ever, tell. She would rather run through the supermarket stark naked and farting than reveal her secret to Mum. This sudden fabulous surprise holiday was going to ruin her life, big-time. Jess's heart sank and sank and sank until it was right down on the carpet like a very ill pet.

But she must try and sound delighted. "Nothing's wrong! I've just got a bit of a headache. But hey, Mum! Thanks! It'll be fantastic! When do we leave?" She tried desperately to force a bit of enthusiasm into her voice, but it was hopeless—like trying to cram her bum into size ten jeans.

"We'll set off the day after tomorrow," said her mum, with the excited smile of a practiced torturer. "Early. There won't be so much traffic then, and we can just potter gently down into the countryside. Oh, I can't wait! It's going to be marvelous!"

Mum's eyes glazed over and she stared out of the window with a look of faraway rapture, as if the angel of the Lord had just appeared over Tesco's. "Ruined abbeys!" she drooled. "Rare wildflowers! Bronze Age burial mounds!"

Jess sometimes thought her mum was slightly off her head. Maybe if her parents had stayed together it would have kept Mum sane. But then again, maybe not. Her dad was kind of crazy too.

"Start packing!" said Mum. "You've only got twenty-four hours!" And she rushed off upstairs, possibly to pack *Fabulous Fossils and Fascinating Cracks in the Ground* or *Sexy Sea Urchins of the South West*.

Twenty-four hours! Jess had to think fast. She had just one day to put an end to this obscene talk of a holiday. Could she become dangerously ill in twenty-four hours? Could she discreetly vandalize the car so it would never, ever, start again? Could she, acting with utmost care of course, slightly burn the house down?

She had to see Fred. Dear Fred! He would know what to do. Perhaps they could elope. Although they had no money. Perhaps they could elope to the bottom of his garden. It was a bit overgrown down there. There was a huge tree. They could secretly live in the tree. A bit like Tarzan and Jane only without the muscles or the beauty.

Darling Fred! She had to text him now! Jess raced up to her bedroom but—how cruel fate was—her mobile phone had disappeared. The floor of her room was covered with a kind of lasagna of clothes, CDs, books, and empty chocolate wrappers. Jess flung the debris around for a moment and then decided to cut her losses and just go round to Fred's house without texting him. He was bound to be there. He almost never went anywhere without telling her, these days.

She just had to check her makeup first. Jess headed for the kitchen, where there was a small mirror above the sink, so you could stare into your own tortured eyes as you washed the dishes. Oh my God, her eyebrows were rubbish. They would have been rubbish even on an orangutan.

Never mind. This was no time to pluck an eyebrow. She flung open the fridge and grabbed a can of Coke. No, wait, that should be water. Although she and Fred were close, they hadn't yet passed the gas barrier. Silent pants were desirable in his company.

Jess got a glass of water and drank it whilst looking in the mirror. Glug, glug, glug went her throat. Like a snake eating a whole family of gerbils. Most unattractive.

"Have you seen my teeth?" came a sudden spooky voice behind her. But it wasn't a spectral presence. It was only Granny. Actually what she said was "Have you feen my teeth?" because when she lost her teeth she couldn't pronounce her s's. She called Jess Jeff. This was slightly irritating. Jess wasn't completely opposed to the idea of a sex change, but if she did unexpectedly become a male person, she wanted to be called Brad, not Jeff.

"Have you looked under your pillow?" asked Jess. They

3

went into Granny's room and found the teeth immediately.

"My goodness, you are brilliant at finding things, dear," said Granny. "You should work in airport security when you leave school."

Jess laughed. Granny's teeth were *always* either in a glass of water on the bedside table or under the pillow.

"No, Granny, I'm going to be a stand-up comedian, remember?" said Jess. "Not as glamorous as airport security, obviously, but somebody's got to perform the backbreaking drudgery of making people laugh."

Granny picked up her teeth and for a moment used them in a kind of ventriloquist act.

"Hello, Jeff!" she said in the squeaky voice she always used for the teeth. "What'f for fupper?" Granny made the teeth chomp together in a hungry kind of way.

This little cabaret had amused Jess quite a lot when she was younger, but now, quite frankly, it was beginning to lose its allure. Jess was desperate to escape and fly to the arms of Fabulous Fred. She laughed politely and backed off down the hallway towards the front door.

"Let's go and watch the news," said Granny, ramming her teeth back into her mouth with panache. "There's been an explosion in Poland, it's terrible. Hundreds feared dead." Granny was quite ghoulish in her addiction to catastrophe.

"I've got to go out, Granny," said Jess, looking at her watch in an important way. "I've got to say goodbye to my friends before I go on holiday."

"Ah! Our lovely trip! I'm so looking forward to it, dear, aren't you? We're going to end up in Cornwall, of course, and that's where Grandpa and I spent our honeymoon, you know."

Jess had heard this story approximately 99,999 times. *Please don't say anything more about it, Granny,* thought Jess desperately, *or I might just have to bundle you away affectionately but briskly into the cupboard under the stairs.*

"And," Granny went on excitedly, "I'm taking Grandpa's ashes so I can throw them into the sea!" Jess smiled through gritted teeth and reached behind her to open the front door.

"Lovely, Granny! Fabulous idea! Ashes, sea—go for it! Kind of like, *The Afterlife Is a Scuba Diving Holiday*!" Granny laughed. She was amazingly broad-minded and would probably laugh at her own funeral.

"Now you must excuse me, Granny—I really must go! Flora's waiting for me in the park!"

"Oh, all right, dear—I'll keep you posted on the Polish explosion when you get back!" promised Granny. She trotted eagerly into the sitting room, heading for the TV. It was already two minutes past five and she might have missed some glorious brand-new disaster. Granny had come to live with them fairly recently and it had certainly brightened things up in the Jordan household. However, right now Jess's thoughts were elsewhere.

She ran out of the house and sped down the road. It had been a lie about Flora waiting for her in the park. An excuse to get away. The person she really had to see was Fred. *Please God,* she prayed as she hurtled off towards the sacred house where the divine Fred Parsons lived. *Save me, please, from this terrible holiday! Sprain my ankle! Sprain both my ankles! And please let Fred be in!*

✳ *2* ✳

Jess
 Jordan   Jess Jordan
Fred Parsons   Jess Parsons
    Fred & Jess Parsons
J. J.   ‼ Flora Parsons ‼

s she ran to Fred's house, Jess tried to get a grip on the situation. But it was totally out of control. The best summer ever had turned into howling darkness in less than half an hour.

Jess and Fred had only just become an item, and they had planned to spend the whole summer together in the park. They were going to have a picnic lunch under a different tree every day. They had even planned some bus trips out of town, to wander through forests or walk hand in hand on a beach "like an insurance ad," as Fred had put it.

And of course, once it got dark, they would probably have spent hours and hours practicing the tiresome business of kissing and cuddling. Every night for the past week, by the park gates, in a private dark place under a tree, Fred

had kissed her goodnight. Jess's skin sort of
memory of it.

"I suppose we'd better go through the who
charade of a goodnight kiss—if we can manage it," Fred
had murmured, the first time. "In fact, I've been chewing
gum all evening in preparation for this moment." He had
spat out his gum—quite stylishly into a rubbish bin—and
they had gone for it.

Their first kiss. It had been long, slow, and delicious.
Jess's heart had gone into overdrive. And eventually, when
they pulled apart, Fred had whispered, "What do you think
of that? Awful, wasn't it?"

"Nauseating!" Jess had sighed, and laid her head on his
heart.

What fatal instinct had made her mum choose this moment to plan a holiday? The very moment when suddenly
just being at home had become heaven on earth? Normally,
of course, Jess would have loved nothing more than to go
down to the seaside and visit her slightly crazy but totally
cute dad, and help him with his rather gloomy paintings of
beaches and seagulls, but just right now . . . the thought
of going away was torture.

It was impossible to tell her mum, hopeless to try and
explain. If Jess even tried she would be in the worst trouble ever. Because Jess's mum wasn't what you'd call boy-
friendly. She wasn't a man-hater exactly, but she only
ever let men into the house if the washing machine wasn't
working.

Jess sometimes thought she would never have the
courage to defy her mum's disapproval and get married.

ιe would have to go and live thousands of miles away in Kalamazoo and pretend her husband was a large dog called Henry.

Jess arrived at Fred's house, panting. She had run all the way. If you want to get fit, don't join a gym—fall in love. She rang the doorbell and tried to put on a casual, glamorous expression, even though her cheeks were bright red and her lungs were wheezing like an old church organ infested with termites.

Fred's father opened the door. Behind him, Jess could hear football on TV. "Is Fred in?" she panted. Fred's dad shook his head.

"He's gone out," he said.

"Oh no! Do you know where he's gone?" cried Jess in dismay. Fred's dad shrugged.

"Sorry," he said in a final kind of way. He didn't invite Jess in to wait till Fred got back. Fred's mum would have known what to do. She would have invited Jess in, offered delicious food and drink, and settled her down to wait with albums full of adorable photos of the infant Fred.

But his dad was a complete duffer. "Excuse me," he said now, as the sound of the football crowd soared in excitement on the TV, "I must get back to the football." And, with a regretful smile, he shut the door in her face.

Jess was devastated, paralyzed, and appalled. Fred's whole street seemed to go dark. Black clouds were gathering, and she had a feeling that vultures were circling overhead. For a moment she was on the verge of tears, but she managed to get rid of them by sort of swallowing the back of her nose. It tasted vile. What should she do now? Where should she go? She was facing disaster, and where was Fred when she needed him? Mysteriously and infuriatingly out.

She only had one hope. She had to go and see her best friend, Flora. Thank goodness Flora hadn't gone on holiday yet. She was due to leave in a couple of days on a "Costa Rican Adventure." Jess wasn't sure exactly where Costa Rica was, but the photos in the brochure suggested that Flora would be trekking through rain forests full of beautiful birds and butterflies and relaxing on tropical beaches under swaying palm trees.

Flora's family could afford such treats because her dad was very big in bathrooms. But this time Jess hadn't felt jealous of Flora's holiday at all, because nothing in the world could be better than just hanging out in the park, all summer, with Fred.

There had been a slightly dodgy moment a few weeks ago, before Jess and Fred had got together, when Flora had revealed that *she* was crazy about Fred. But once Fred had confessed his perverted preference for dark, imperfect Jess rather than blond, perfect Flora, Flora had dug deep into her character and produced an unsuspected angelic streak. She had only sulked about it for three days.

Jess broke into a run. She desperately needed some sympathy and Flora was usually very prompt with the hugs and hot chocolate.

The front door was opened by Flora's older sister, Freya. Freya was at Oxford studying maths and sex appeal. Like all Flora's family, she was blond and almost illegally beautiful. She was kind of vague and dreamy as well, which somehow added to her angelic charm. If Jess had tried to be vague and dreamy it wouldn't have worked. She would just have appeared overweight and retarded.

"Oh—er—hello, Jess," murmured Freya. "Flora's . . . where is Flora? Er, yes, um, I think she's in the sitting room with Mummy. . . ." And she drifted off to do some very hard sums or possibly rinse her hair in extract of chamomile flowers. Jess took off her shoes (one always had to do this at Flora's, as if it was a mosque) and tiptoed to the sitting room. How soon would she be able to get Flora on her own and cry on her shoulder?

But an amazing sight met Jess's startled gaze. Flora's mother, who on a good day could pass for a low-budget Madonna, was lying on the sofa with a badly bruised cheekbone and a black eye, and with her leg in plaster! What on earth had happened? It seemed that Jess would be expected to provide sympathy instead of receiving it. How unfair life was!

"Come in, Jess, darling, don't be scared, although I
do look like something out of a horror movie!"
called Flora's mum. Flora was sitting on the
floor by the sofa. You could see she had been crying for
hours. Her eyes had gone pink and piggy. Although of
course she still looked a lot more beautiful than Jess, whose
eyes were piggy every day of the year.

"What's happened?" said Jess, sitting down on the floor
beside Flora.

"I had a stupid fall when I was getting out of the bath,"
said Flora's mum. "It was that slippery bath oil—rose gera-
nium."

"I gave it to her for her birthday!" said Flora. "It's all my
fault! Mum's broken her leg and we've had to cancel the
holiday and everything."

"Oh no!" cried Jess in dismay. She knew how much Flora had been looking forward to wandering through the Cloud Forest and admiring the howler monkeys.

"Never mind, darling." Mrs. Barclay stroked Flora's hair. "Jess has come to cheer you up! Haven't you, Jess?" Jess nodded as cheerfully as possible. It was, however, the very opposite of what she had come for. Flora was supposed to be cheering *her* up, dammit!

How ironical. Flora was devastated because her holiday had gone down the toilet: Jess's life had gone down the toilet because of an unwanted holiday. Jess had to stop thinking like this. She was starting to want to *go to* the toilet.

"So how's your mother?" inquired Flora's mum. Flora stared tragically at the carpet. It was clearly Jess's job to transform the mood of the party from deep gloom to ecstasy with a few well-chosen witticisms about her mother, of all things.

"Well, Mum's excited," she began, without much inspiration. "We're going on a . . ." Jess paused. Was it tactless to mention her own holiday? She hesitated. ". . . a kind of a trip . . . mainly to see my dad."

"A trip!" Flora's mum's eyes lit up. "How lovely for you, Jess! Your father lives in St. Ives, doesn't he! Oh, I adore St. Ives! All those beaches! All that art! You'll have such a fabulous time."

"I'm not sure about that," said Jess doubtfully. "My mum and dad don't exactly get on. And Granny's coming with us. She wants to throw my grandpa's ashes into the sea."

"Oh, bless her, what a wonderful idea!" Flora's mum's voice softened slightly, acquiring semitragic overtones.

"How romantic and yet terribly sad. I would like to be thrown into the sea, Flora, when the time comes—now don't forget, darling."

Flora looked, for an instant, as if she would like to throw her mother into the sea right now. Or possibly herself. There are times so hard that you're torn between homicide and suicide, and Flora was clearly in just such a dilemma.

"So you're going on a lovely kind of tour! What's your route going to be?" asked Flora's mum.

"I'm not sure . . . it's a very last-minute thing," admitted Jess. "Mum did mention ruined abbeys and stuff."

"Ruined abbeys!" cried Flora's mum in rapture, as if she would like one on toast right now. "Doesn't that sound marvelous, Flora! Isn't Jess lucky!"

Flora roused herself from her deep depression, reached across, and squeezed Jess's hand. "Yeah, I'm glad you're going to have a fun time, babe," she said. But there was a strange sort of sighing sound in her voice. Her own tragic failure to go on holiday was clearly a lot more interesting than Jess's tiresome ruined abbeys.

Jess's own modest little tragedy had been totally outclassed by Flora's family crisis. Flora's family was, as usual, superior. Even their disasters were more glamorous than hers, dammit.

Flora's mum moved slightly on the sofa, and winced with pain. "Ow! Ow! Oh dear! I'm useless!" she said. Jess couldn't help feeling a bit jealous. It seemed such a waste of a broken leg—causing Flora's mother so much distress. Jess would have welcomed a broken leg with open arms—as it were.

Immediately Jess tried to think of loads of lovely fun things that Flora's mum could still enjoy, even with a broken leg. It wasn't a very long list. "It might be a good excuse to do jigsaws," suggested Jess hesitantly.

"Oh, I adore jigsaws!" cried Flora's mum. The woman was so determined to be positive that even if Jess had suggested bungee jumping, she was sure that plucky Mrs. Barclay would have signed up for a session right away.

"What a brilliant idea! Let's get the Royal Family jigsaw out!" said Flora's mum, and Flora went off to get it. Her little sister, Felicity, then appeared, carrying her flute.

"Mum, will you listen to my flute solo and tell me if it's all right? I've been practicing for ages and I can't get the middle section fast enough."

"Of course, darling!" said Mrs. Barclay. And this was the fatal moment when the evening kind of solidified into awfulness. Jess just had to grit her teeth and get through it.

Instead of pouring her heart out to Flora and receiving massive amounts of tender loving care and sympathy, she spent an eternity listening over and over again to Felicity's extremely dull flute solo whilst looking in vain among hundreds of jigsaw pieces for the Queen's teeth.

It was almost a relief to be out alone on the pavements, walking home afterwards in the dark. At least she could wallow in her own misery and not be required to make sparkling conversation with people even worse off than herself.

Tomorrow she would have to start packing. And she hadn't even had a chance to break the news to Fred yet. The streetlamps had come on, and rather grim little pools of light punctuated the deep shade of the trees that lined the avenue. Jess was about a hundred yards from her front gate when a hooded figure stepped out from the shadows and barred her path.

Oh my God! She was going to be mugged! The perfect end to a day of unparalleled vileness. The figure towered above her, his face blotted out because of the streetlamp behind him. Jess's heart leapt in panic and she saw huge headlines in tomorrow's paper: SCHOOLGIRL MURDERED WITHIN 100 YARDS OF HER FRONT GATE. *Help me, God!* She uttered a silent, desperate prayer. *I'll enjoy every minute of that lovely history tour with my mum, if only you'll let me live.*

The figure grabbed her arm. "Hey, not so fast!" came a harsh, rasping voice. "You don't escape so easily. I, the Hooded Horror, must first drink your hot blood."

It was Fred.

4

Fred

*J*ess was swept up into a gigantic hug. "I've been hanging about here," growled Fred into her hair, "for three hours. I'm on all the CCTV footage. Prime suspect for all the major crimes round here. Where have you been, for God's sake? Flirting with lover boy?"

Jess giggled into his shirt. Fred could make her laugh even in moments of the deepest gloom—which, let's face it, just about described the situation right now.

"Who's lover boy?" she demanded indignantly.

"Ben Jones, of course," said Fred. "I know you still secretly long for him. You're dying to run your fingers through his beautiful blond football-captain's hair. Admit it!"

"What utter crap, Fred!" said Jess. "You're lover boy these days—or hadn't you noticed? Ben was just a very old crush. *So* last season. Besides, I actually came round your house at five o'clock, looking for you—and you were out. So where the hell were you? Giving extra English lessons to Jodie?"

"Aha!" said Fred mysteriously. "I was out in town, arranging a very special treat for you." He released her from his arms, reached inside his jacket, and produced a glamorous white envelope.

Jess knew, at the back of her mind, that she must tell Fred the bad news about her enforced holiday with her stupid family, but she couldn't bear to mention it yet. Whenever she was with Fred they had the best time. Right now, he was waving the white envelope above her head. Jess jumped up a couple of times, laughing and trying to snatch it, but Fred was so much taller, he just reached up and it was way out of Jess's reach.

"It's rather like training a small but eager dog," he said mockingly. "Shall we go walkies?"

"Give me the envelope," said Jess, "or I'll morph completely into a cute little dog and pee on your shoes!"

"Sweet!" said Fred with a grin. "Tempting. But OK . . . you can have the envelope. It'll cost you . . . hmm, one kiss, though." Jess launched herself eagerly back into his arms.

She had read somewhere that you shouldn't throw yourself at boys. It was best to preserve an elegant sort of mystery and poise. That was how you would retain your allure, or something. Jess knew for sure that her allure was zilch. Her only hope of retaining Fred's interest was to grab him and cling to him and never let him go. So completely without mystery or poise, they kissed.

It was a humdinger. Five minutes later they broke apart

for breath. In an ideal world they would have had access to a halftime shower, a pep talk from the coach, and some high-energy sport glucose drink. But none of these was available: just a dark, deserted street.

The kiss had completely wiped from Jess's mind everything else in the world: the envelope and her awful news. Maybe her mother was right about relationships with men destroying one's brain. Jess looked up at Fred and Fred looked down at Jess. He widened his eyes and made a soft hooting noise like a baby owl. They had always imitated animals and birds to each other, all their lives, since they were little kids at playgroup.

Then he produced the white envelope, and with a formal bow, presented it to her. Jess was vastly intrigued. Her hands trembled slightly. There was something so white, so beautiful and crisp about it. It glimmered in the street-lamps, full of promise.

Jess tried to open it very gently and elegantly, with poise and allure. But her little finger sort of got stuck under the flap, so in the end she ripped it open with an impatient yell. Inside were two tickets to something . . . for a moment Jess couldn't quite make it out in the gloom. Then she saw the words *Riverdene Festival*. Oh my God! It was the music event to die for! All Jess's favorite bands were going to be there!

"It's two tickets for Riverdene," said Fred. "I thought we could elope there next week. I've been saving up for months, working in the newsagents on Sunday mornings, and stashing away my gold in a strongbox under my bed. My mum says we can borrow one of our tents—or if your mum's not happy about us sharing a tent, we can take two. Just to keep her quiet. So. What do you say?"

Jess was dumbstruck. She couldn't think of anything more amazing than going to Riverdene with Fred. But what catastrophic timing! Her heart seemed to crack and crumble. It was hopeless. But Fred was looking at her with such happy, shiny eyes that she couldn't bear to disappoint him. So for a moment it was impossible to say anything at all.

"You're right to hesitate, of course," he said, filling the silence, but there was a slight edge of worry in his voice. He speeded up. "The thought of spending several days in a field with thousands of unwashed kids would fill anyone with dismay. Of course. Perhaps it's the idea of proximity with me which is causing you a moment's hesitation? Let me assure you that, if you require it, I will happily pitch my tent five hundred yards away. I will only speak to you from a respectful distance. Or possibly even send a note."

Jess laughed, but her face was filling up with secret tears again. Poor, dear Fred! This lovely surprise of his made her bad news so much worse. "And if the discomforts of open-air living are a cause for concern," Fred continued, "let me assure you that the long-range weather forecast is fine. Though personally I have a sneaking regard for rain. Indeed, I feel it is a very underrated weather pattern and possibly its time will come, though not, I hope, while we are at Riverdene."

Still Jess said nothing. But a tear slid down her cheek. Fred put his arm round her shoulders. "What's wrong?" he asked. It was very unusual for Fred to speak in such a short sentence. He had clearly begun to sense the crisis. Jess looked up at him and shook her head dolefully. "I can't think of anything more wonderful," she said. "This is so sweet of you, Fred. To use up all your savings like that and organize this brilliant, brilliant surprise for me. But there's a problem."

"What?" said Fred, urgently. He had uttered only one word. He was clearly already deeply troubled and he hadn't even heard the worst of it yet.

"My mum informed me this afternoon that she's taking me away on a holiday the day after tomorrow," said Jess. Fred's shoulders slumped. He suddenly looked only about five seven instead of his usual five eleven. He said . . . nothing. For Fred to be speechless was, perhaps, a first in the history of the world.

* 5 *

"What's worse," sobbed Jess, "is that we're going to be away for ages—it could be weeks." It wasn't very attractive, this crying business. Her eyes filled with tears, but somehow, so did her nose. "Sorry," she said. "I'm being disgusting."

Fred reached up into the tree and picked a leaf. He offered it to her. "Wipe your nose on this," he suggested. Jess tried, but the leaf wasn't quite as absorbent as she had hoped, and only spread slime all over her face. She threw it away. Even Nature seemed against them.

"Here," said Fred. He pulled his shirt up and tenderly wiped her face with it. "Don't cry," he said quietly. "It's all right." He drew her close to him. She laid her head against his chest.

"Don't cry anymore," he said quietly. "It's quite all right. I'll just . . . I'll just have to take Jodie, that's all."

"Fred! You pig!" Jess freed herself and whirled round, grabbed his shirt, and shook him. They wrestled playfully for a moment or two. He was laughing, but more in desperation than anything.

"Just a joke, just a joke!" he said. "I wouldn't share a tent with Jodie if I was in Antarctica and my survival depended on it!"

"It's not very funny, though, is it?" sighed Jess. "What a totally vile scenario. Everything's against us."

"Well, at least our families aren't involved in a blood feud," said Fred. They had watched the video of *Romeo and Juliet* quite recently. "My mother thinks you're some kind of princess. In fact, I think she would gladly swap me for you in part-exchange if you were available on eBay."

"Your mum is so cool," sighed Jess.

"Well, she clearly thinks that you're my only chance of staying out of jail," said Fred. "I don't suppose you've told your mum about us yet?"

He looked just a tiny bit irritated. It was getting to be a bit of an issue between them, to be honest.

Jess sighed. She was glad Fred's mother liked her, and indeed she herself adored the dear lady. But whilst her own mum had no objection to Fred as an individual, if she knew he had become Jess's boyfriend, she would immediately reclassify him as vermin and set a boy trap by the front door baited with a large piece of cheese.

"What sort of holiday is it?" asked Fred. "Is it already booked and everything?"

"I don't think so," said Jess, "knowing my mum. She's very last-minute. She's got this obsession about taking me on a tour through England and torturing me with history and botany and stuff. We're heading for St. Ives, down in Cornwall, to see my dad."

"Ah! Your dad!" said Fred. "But you've been wanting to go down and see him for ages. In fact, you've bored me to death with the subject recently. And I'm sure the eccentric old chap would love to see you." Fred pondered for a moment, then brightened. "Hey! Maybe, if it's not all finalized yet, your mum wouldn't mind leaving a few days later. So we could go to Riverdene first," said Fred. But he didn't sound very convinced. "At least ask her. Explain the situation. Remind her of my many sterling qualities."

"I'll ask her," said Jess with a heavy heart. "But don't expect a miracle."

"Well," said Fred, "my advice is, go home, do the washing up, and tell her she's the best mum in the world. Unfortunately the florists are all closed, but as you said, the world is against us. You could try presenting Riverdene as an educational experience."

Jess sighed. "I'll try," she said. "But to be honest, I don't think there's a chance in hell of her saying yes."

"Never mind," said Fred. "Just give it your best shot. And text me as soon as you get her reaction. I'll have to go home and watch something of unsurpassed violence on TV. Ah, where would we be without our visual comfort food? Tarantino, here I come! But first, may I suggest . . . the goodnight kiss?"

Ten minutes later Jess detached herself, most reluctantly, from Fred's arms. "Send me a text tonight," he whispered. "I'll be waiting with ludicrous eagerness."

"OK," said Jess. "Although I'll have to find my mobile first."

Jess ran the hundred yards or so to her front gate. When she reached her house she looked back. Fred was standing under a streetlight, watching her. He raised his hand and waved. A little throb of adoration ran through her.

God, he even waved more sweetly than anybody else in the world! She tore her eyes away, trudged up her front path with a sinking feeling, and, having discovered that she'd forgotten her keys, she rang the doorbell.

Five seconds later the door was thrown open by her mum. She was actually quivering with rage.

"Where the hell have you been?" she yelled. "Look at the time! It's ten past eleven! You disappeared at five o'clock and I've heard absolutely nothing since! Not a call, not a text—nothing! For all I knew you'd been strangled! Lying in a ditch somewhere! I've been absolutely beside myself!"

"Sorry," said Jess meekly, and shot indoors past her mum as fast as possible, cringing like a dog expecting to be whipped. Her mother would never dream of laying a finger on her, of course—but with a ferocious tongue like hers, a verbal beating-up was far more effective anyway. "I've just been at Flora's, that's all," said Jess.

"Get to bed!" snapped her mother. "I don't want to hear another word! You'll be the death of me! I do my very best to look after you, love you, care for you, plan treats for you, and what do I get in return? A kick in the teeth."

"Sorry, Mum," said Jess from the top of the stairs. "I'm really sorry." It didn't seem the right moment to launch the tricky subject of Riverdene. And it didn't seem likely that the right moment would arrive for weeks, months, or even years.

* 6 *

LIESLIESLIESLIESLIESLIES

*J*ess came down in the morning very bleary-eyed. She had slept badly and had dreamed that she'd microwaved a friend's pet gerbil in a moment of absentmindedness. It wasn't the ideal start to the day.

Mum was glowering at the breakfast table. Granny was smiling serenely over a newspaper account of a man who had run amok in a garden center with a stainless-steel spade.

Jess kissed the top of Granny's head and put her arm round her mum. "Don't try and soft-soap me," said Mum. "I'm still very cross about last night."

"Never let the sun set on your anger, Madeleine," said Granny. A bit rich, coming from a woman whose chief interest in life was murder.

"I'm really sorry, Mum," said Jess, plugging her mobile into the charger. She had finally found it, under a pile of music magazines on her bedroom floor. It needed charging—another sign of the hostility of the universe.

"The only reason I didn't ring you was my mobile had run out of charge." The first lie of the morning. Although it wasn't such a terribly wicked lie—her mobile *had* run out of charge, after all. It was just that Jess hadn't had it with her last night. So it was a lie containing a tasty little nugget of truth, like one of those chocolates with a nut in the middle. Jess felt that at least she'd got off to a flying lying start, and helped herself to a bowl of cornflakes.

"You could have rung from Flora's," said Mum with a glare. Jess could not deny it. She just shrugged and tried hard to look contrite. "I'm really, really sorry," she said, crunching the cornflakes as innocently as possible. "I'll never do it again."

"Huh!" said her mum. She got up from the table, cleared away her plate, and started to pack. She put a pile of guides and maps into a cardboard box marked Baked Beans. *My family is so* trashy, thought Jess. *I wish we had lovely old distinguished leather suitcases like Flora's family has.*

Jess was wondering how on earth she was ever going to broach the subject of Fred and Riverdene. Maybe she would just never find the necessary courage.

"So how is Flora?" asked Granny, perhaps hoping that, since they had last met, Flora might have been arrested for a homicide.

"Oh, she's more or less heartbroken," said Jess. "They've had to cancel that fabulous holiday in Costa Rica. Her mum's broken her leg."

"What?" Jess's mum stopped packing. "Oh no! Oh dear! That lovely holiday! How terrible! How did it happen?"

"She slipped in the bathroom," said Jess. She was relieved that at last they were talking about something other than her own crimes. "Getting out of the bath."

"How awful! And poor Flora! She was so much looking forward to that holiday!" said Mum again, looking devastated. Jess was beginning to get irritated. OK, it was fine to feel sympathy for Flora's canceled holiday, sure, but Jess wouldn't have minded a little motherly sympathy for her own tragic dilemma. Although, come to think of it, her mum *was* her own tragic dilemma.

"Yeah," she agreed. "Poor Flora." Then suddenly a brilliant, brilliant idea shot across her mind, like a jet-propelled banana. "But we've hatched a plot to cheer her up."

"What?"

"Well, she's invited me to go to Riverdene," announced Jess with a daring, reckless flash of genius. Mum wouldn't object to Jess going with Flora, surely. She could secretly go with Fred, but pretend she was going with Flora. Flora would play ball. She must! After all, Jess had lied to Flora's dad hundreds of times last term when Flora was going out with Mackenzie.

"But surely Riverdene's next week?"

"Yes, but . . ." Jess reached deep into her store of charming persuasion. "If we went on our trip a bit later, that would give Flora and me time to go to Riverdene, yeah? I mean, it would give you more time to do your research into ruined abbeys. And it would *so* cheer Flora up."

Jess's mum hesitated. You could see she was going to say no, but she was just gathering her arguments together.

27

"It's out of the question," she said. "For a start, those tickets cost a fortune."

"Flora's already got the tickets," said Jess recklessly. "She says she'd be happy to pay for me—as a sort of early birthday present. It would be so nice for Flora to have something to cheer her up, Mum. You could see yesterday she'd been crying for ages. Her eyes were all red."

Although Jess's mum was 95 percent against the whole idea, it was as if 5 percent of her felt so sorry for Flora, she might just postpone her own holiday in Flora's honor.

Jess waited, on tenterhooks. It had been a crazy impulse to disguise Fred's offer as Flora's offer, but it just might work. If her mum said yes, she'd obviously have to call Flora right away to make sure she was fully briefed, in case her mum rang Flora's mum. In fact, come to think of it, Flora really might have to come along to Riverdene too, as a sort of smoke screen.

Goddammit! Things were getting more and more complicated. Jess loved Flora, and Jess loved Fred. But what if Flora started flirting with him?

What if, as they sat around a campfire, Flora's eyes met Fred's through a hazy drift of smoke? What if the strings of his heart went ZING and he realized in a flash that it was Flora he loved, not Jess?

"It's out of the question," said Jess's mum. Jess was almost relieved. After the horrible hallucination she had just had about Flora and Fred round the campfire, she suddenly didn't fancy the idea of Riverdene quite so much. And anyway, she was now in such hot water, having lied to her mum so recklessly, that she just wanted to change the subject to anything else, to anything in the whole wide world.

"OK, OK," she said. "I didn't expect you to say yes. Fine. OK. Forget I ever mentioned it. So, Granny—how many people did that guy kill with the spade?"

"Still, I'd better just ring Flora's mother," said Mum, with a sudden disastrous lurch into politeness. "I ought to apologize for the fact that you can't go to Riverdene. And I must offer my sympathy about the accident."

"No!" cried Jess in dismay. "Don't ring!"

Her mum stopped and looked at her with deep suspicion. "Why not?" she demanded. Jess's mind went blank, and she began to gibber. Oh God! Why had she ever told that stupid lie?

"Because she was saying . . . Flora's mum was saying yesterday that she's just fed up with people ringing up to express their sympathy. It makes her feel so much worse." Catastrophically, Jess blushed at the feebleness of her own excuse. Knowing Jess very well, her mum saw the blush and smelt a rat.

Very firmly, she pushed past Jess, picked up the phone, and dialed Flora's number.

"What's the time, dear?" asked Granny irrelevantly, from somewhere on a different planet. Jess sighed. It was time to run for cover. Because the poo was about to hit the air-conditioning unit.

* 7 *

It was time for silent, urgent praying—again. Mum waited for Flora's mother to pick up the phone, and all the time she was glaring at Jess. Jess tried to look casual and confident, but she was secretly making urgent plans to escape within seconds—possibly to run up to the bathroom and flush herself down the toilet.

"Mrs. Barclay?" said her mum suddenly. Jess's heart gave a sickening lurch. "Oh, sorry, Freya: you sound just like your mum. I was so sorry to hear she's had this dreadful accident." Thank goodness Jess hadn't lied about that bit.

"Might it be possible for me to have a word with her?" asked Jess's mum. "Oh, I see . . . I'll try again later, then. Thanks a lot. Bye!"

Jess's mum put the phone down. "She's having a bath," said Mum. "Of course it takes a bit of time, with her leg in plaster and everything, and there's a nurse come to help her, so she's not available for half an hour or so."

Jess knew she must disguise her intense relief as relaxed indifference. "I suppose I'd better start packing," she said. She had to ring Flora right away, to warn her. She just hoped her mobile was fully charged by now. She ripped it out of the socket, with desperate, urgent casualness.

"I've got a bit of packing to finish too," said Mum, and went upstairs. Damn! It would now be virtually impossible for Jess to phone Flora from her bedroom without being overheard. "I think I'll just go for a little walk to the corner shop first," called Jess. "I need some chewing gum."

"No! Pack first!" insisted her mum, glaring down the stairs at her. "I'm not having you running around all over town, and me not knowing where you are. I've had enough of that, Jess. Come up here and pack!"

Jess shrugged sweetly, even though she was longing to hurl a wet sponge or raw burger into her mother's face. She went upstairs to her bedroom, closed the door, and listened. How soundproof was it? She could clearly hear her mother moving around. So her mum would have no problem hearing every word Jess said to Flora.

Jess put on her Slipknot album (the loudest CD in the world), dived under her duvet, and switched on her mobile. It bleeped excitedly. What now? A text from Fred and one from Dad! Oh God! They'd have to wait! Frantically Jess dialed Flora's mobile. "Hi!" said Flora. Thank God! She was picking up. Jess had to explain. And fast.

"Listen, Flo, thisiscrucial. My mumsgonnaringyourmum and ask her about Riverdene!"

"What? Did you say Riverdene?" said Flora, rather stupidly.

"Yeah! You've gottapretendyouandI have been planningtogothere…"

Suddenly the deafening noise of Slipknot suddenly stopped, and Jess heard her mum's voice in the room, right next to the bed. Nightmare!

"What the hell's going on, Jess?" she demanded. Jess just had time to press the OFF button and thrust her mobile under the pillow before her mum ripped the covers off. "What are you doing under the duvet?" What indeed? Jess's mind whirled, desperate for a convincing reason why she might have been in this rather unusual posture.

"Sounds kind of silly, Mum, but I'm doing these exercises to train myself not to be scared of the dark." Her mum gave her a deeply suspicious glare.

"You're up to something, I can tell," she said. "I've got my eye on you, my girl. Now get on with your packing— and no music! I don't want any more of that infernal racket!" And she stalked off—but she didn't close the door behind her.

Jess decided she'd better not do anything so obvious and guilty as closing her bedroom door right away, so she started packing, humming to herself in an innocent kind of way—the sort of song that pure, angelic milkmaids might sing as they tripped through the dewy fields at dawn.

But she had to get another message to Flora. Their mums could be talking on the phone any second now and Flora had to be fully briefed. Jess grabbed her mobile and whizzed off a text. I TOLD MUM WE WERE PLANNING TO GO

TO RIVERDENE—FOR GOD'S SAKE BACK ME UP. I TOLD HER YOU ALREADY HAD THE TICKETS. SORRY!

Jess wouldn't abbreviate her texts, on principle, even at times like this. She fancied herself as a literary princess and prided herself on being able to text very long words at the speed of light.

About five minutes later the house phone rang. Jess jumped in terror. Granny called up the stairs, "Madeleine! It's Flora's mother!"

"Right! I'll take it up here in my study!" Mum answered. Jess listened, her heart racing like the rhythm section of a samba band.

"Hello!" she heard her mum say, in her slightly posh telephone voice. "I just wanted to talk to you about this plan the girls have cooked up about going to Riverdene. Has Flora mentioned anything about it?" Then there was a long pause while Jess's mum listened to whatever it was Flora's mum was saying.

The next thing Jess's mum said would be crucial. If she sounded relaxed, Flora would have got the message and Jess would have escaped by the skin of her teeth. If Jess's mum sounded angry, Jess would be hurled into a black pit of evildoing and be pronged to death by devils in red Lycra.

"Ah, I see. I thought as much . . . No, I agree absolutely. Of course they're too young. And besides, I'm taking Jess away on holiday tomorrow, so it would have been out of the question anyway." She didn't sound furious. Just mildly irritated. Jess felt a wave of relief.

"Yes, I was so sorry to hear about that," her mum went on. "You must all be very disappointed."

Jess could hear her mum winding up the phone call. Moments later she came straight into Jess's room without knocking. "I've sorted that, then," she said. "Sorry, love, but you and Flora are just not old enough to go to Riverdene. Maybe next year, OK?"

"Yeah, OK, fair enough, Mum," said Jess, feeling relieved. She seemed to have escaped from the dreadful sticky web of lies. Just.

All she had to do now was tell Fred the sad news that Riverdene was off. The minute her mum was out of the room, Jess pounced on the texts from Fred and her dad. Fred had sent his late last night. WHAT'S HAPPENING IN THE WAR ZONE? IS THERE NO HOPE? SHALL WE ELOPE? I CAN'T POSSIBLY SLEEP UNTIL I'VE HEARD FROM YOU. ZZZZZZZ . . . SNORE . . .

Poor Fred! Jess felt terribly guilty that she hadn't been able to text him last night. She must keep her phone in her pocket, always, from now on, and never lose it again. The text from Dad was one of his usual wacky wisecracking messages.

DEAR CHILD, I HEAR YOU ARE COMING DOWN TO CORNWALL TO SEE ME. I AM THRILLED TO BITS. COUNTING THE DAYS. HASTILY TRIMMING MY NOSTRIL HAIR AND SCRAPING THE COBWEBS OFF MY FACE. HAVE YOU GROWN MUCH SINCE EASTER? TEMPTED TO PAINT THE WHOLE HOUSE PINK IN HONOR OF YOUR ARRIVAL. LURVE, THE DAD.

Jess felt guilty about this text too. Her dad was being so lovable and excited about the prospect of her visit—and she would have moved heaven and earth to stay right here at home!

Drained by this unexpected double dose of guilt, she could not face answering either of the texts. Somehow she had to tell Fred that Riverdene was off, and that she had to leave with her mum tomorrow. But she couldn't tell him by text. It would be too cruel. It would have to be in person. She whizzed off a text. SEE YOU AT 7 BY THE PARK GATE? The answer came straight back.

WHAT'S HAPPENING? WHY DIDN'T YOU TEXT ME LAST NIGHT? SEEMS AGES SINCE WE LAST MET. CAN'T REMEMBER WHAT YOU LOOK LIKE. JUST REMIND ME—WHO ARE YOU AGAIN? Jess was suddenly brokenhearted all over again at the thought of the fabulous time she and Fred would have had at the festival. And if twelve hours' separation was unbearable—what would two or three weeks be like? But there seemed to be no way out.

Still, Fred would understand. And they'd be able to keep in touch. There'd be cybercafes. Maybe they could chat online as well as by phone. And she would send him a postcard every day. Maybe even whole long letters.

It was nearly lunchtime when the phone rang again. They were all downstairs. Jess was laying the table, her mum was fixing some soup, and Granny was reading the murder trial reports.

"Oh, who on earth's that?" said Mum. "Someone always rings up when I'm cooking. Keep your eye on this soup, Jess. Don't let it boil." She walked over and picked up the phone.

"Hello? Madeleine Jordan speaking."

Jess stirred the soup, and turned it down. But right away she noticed there was something odd about her mum's

35

body language. Something bad. "What?" said Mum. "*What? I see* . . . No, no, I can assure you this is news to me. It explains a lot, though." And she turned round and gave Jess a glare that could have grilled bacon at three yards.

"There's been a murder in Bognor," said Granny, irrelevantly. Jess quailed. It seemed as if there might be a murder a lot nearer home, any minute now.

"No, I'm sorry, but it's out of the question," her mum said, quite snappily, to whoever it was on the phone. Jess's mind whirled blindly. She couldn't imagine who it was. She just knew she was deeply submerged in elephant poo, right up to her chin.

"I don't think Jess is nearly old enough, and besides, we're leaving for a family holiday tomorrow. . . . That's OK. . . . Bye!" Her mum slammed down the phone and turned to confront Jess, her eyes spitting rage.

"That was Fred's mother," she said, "asking if I'd prefer you to take two tents rather than one to Riverdene, and offering her spare one. Very considerate of her, wasn't it?"

* 8 *

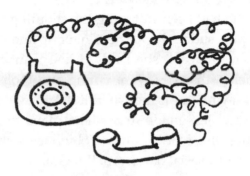

*J*ess opened her mouth to try and protest, but her mum had only paused for breath, and dived back in. "So it was Fred's idea to go to the festival—he's the one who's got the tickets—and you didn't have the guts to tell me."

"We were all going!" shouted Jess. "Loads of us! OK, it was Fred's idea in the first place. But the whole gang was involved: Flora, Jodie . . ." For an instant Jess was so panicked, her mind went blank and she couldn't remember the names of any of her friends. So she invented some. "Gloria, Toby, Hamish, Max, Cleo . . . Ben J., Ben S., Ben . . . X.—"

"I've never heard of any of these people!" yelled her mum. "For all I know they could be drug dealers or something! Why do you have to sneak around doing things

37

behind my back all the time? I never know what's going on and you never come clean!"

"You're the one who never comes clean!" exploded Jess. "I've been asking you for years why you and Dad split up and I never get a straight answer!"

Granny, who had been watching the shouting match like a tennis umpire, suddenly put her finger up and in the brief silence which followed, she said, "I just want to remind you, Madeleine, that you were young and foolish once—not that I'm saying Jess is foolish, mind."

Dear Granny! Jess made immediate plans to name her first child after her. Not "Granny," obviously—that would be something of a social handicap. But Granny's first name, Valerie, would surely come back into fashion sooner or later. Jess's mother gave Granny an exasperated glance, and shot a last ferocious glare at Jess.

"I'm certainly not going to waste the rest of the day bickering. Go upstairs and finish your packing, Jess. We all need an early night."

It seemed as if Jess would have to abandon her plans for a secret meeting with Fred at seven o'clock by the park gates. She went up to her room and sent him a text.

AS YOU'LL HAVE GATHERED, MUM ASCENDED THE NEAREST WALL. SORRY. NO HOPE OF GETTING OUT TONIGHT. BE GOOD WHILE I'M AWAY, AND FOR GOD'S SAKE TEXT ME DAILY.

Instantly the reply came back. MY HEART HAS BROKEN WITH A SICKENING CRACK AUDIBLE IN ICELAND. I'LL SELL THE RIVERDENE TICKETS AND BUY LOADS OF VIO-LENT VIDEOS INSTEAD. WRITE ME A LETTER NOW AND

THEN, OK? LUCKILY I WON'T HAVE TO REPLY AS YOU WON'T HAVE A FIXED ADDRESS. Jess felt slightly comforted by the thought of writing Fred letters. She started one straightaway.

Dear Fred,

This is the first of a series of letters describing the horrors of travel in the 21st century. I am upstairs in my tragic little bedroom, packing. I'm only packing black clothes, of course. I shall be in mourning throughout this damned trip. I shall pose picturesquely against haunted ruins, at sunset, with ravens in my hair, utterly deranged and occasionally muttering "Fred . . . Fred . . ."

It's a shame you haven't got a slightly more tragic name. I mean, Fred. Not much grandeur there. I think I shall rename you. How about Archibald? Or would you prefer Hamlet? Hamlet Parsons—it has a certain ring.

I'm bracing myself for an early start. My mum has OD'd on history guidebooks and I dread what's in store. "Jess, are you listening? Here is the stone where King Egbert the Hard—boiled was mashed up with mayonnaise by the Vikings in the year 809. And this is the tower where St. Kylie received the Sacred Acne.

"In this garden Prince Flatulent proposed to

39

Lady Isabel Ginger—Niblets in 1678. And this flower commemorates their love, as well as being a cure for severe halitosis. It's called the Lesser Spotted Stinkweed. Rub some on your gums and feel it tingle!"

So, my dear Hamlet, tomorrow morning I shall be wrenched away from the divine city where you live. I shall be dragged screaming off down country lanes infested with thundering herds of squirrels and things.

But you—you will be left here undefended against evil. Beautiful girls will pass you in the street, giving you saucy sidelong glances. They will sort of accidentally brush up against you in the hip—hop section of the sinisterly named Virgin Megastore. They will be playing tennis sexily whenever you walk in the park, flashing their bronzed elbows seductively in the sunshine. How will you ever hold out?

There was one local girl in particular that Jess was worried about. Flora, of course. She and Fred might not need the romantic setting of a campfire at a festival. They might just bump into each other in the High Street, go for a coffee, and one thing might lead to another.

Eventually Jess prayed briefly for God to smite all the local girls with boils, and make Flora smell like a rubbish bin full of rotting cabbage—just for the duration of Jess's holiday. Then she fell into an uneasy sleep.

* 9 *

ext day they started early. Normally at 8:15 a.m. (in the holidays, anyway) Jess would have been turning over in bed and sinking luxuriously into a dream about being chased around dark city streets by an ape in a tutu. But today, by 8:15 a.m. they were already driving down the motorway.

"Oh, look at the sky! Have you ever seen such blue!" cried Jess's mum hysterically. Her normal character, mostly stern and anxious, seemed to have been replaced by a disconcerting, deranged joy.

This happened occasionally when her mum had a chance to wallow in Nature or History. History and Nature were clearly going to loom large on this trip. Jess sighed.

"Blue is my favorite color!" Mum went on, as if she hadn't already done it justice. "So many lovely things are blue. Sapphires . . . The sea . . ."

"What's your favorite color, Jess?" asked Granny from the front passenger seat.

"Black," said Jess. She was dressed from head to toe in black.

"Oh, that black thing is just a phase!" said her mum. "You'll grow out of it." Jess made immediate plans to wear nothing but black for the rest of her life. She would even get married in black (if indeed she ever got married). She would wear a long dress in black satin, carry a bouquet of black flowers, wear jet earrings and a deep black veil, and on her shoulder would be her pet raven called Nero.

Fred would wear white, though. She hoped it would be Fred she was marrying, anyway. She certainly couldn't imagine herself ever marrying anyone else. Yes, Fred would wear a white suit, white shoes, and a white rose in his buttonhole. And possibly, for that final little weird touch, white contact lenses.

Jess spent the next hour fantasizing about marrying Fred. Their wedding day would be at Christmas, so he would never forget their anniversary, and the buffet would include deep-fried mince pies.

"The ancient Britons and the Celts both worshipped the horse," said her mum suddenly, just as Jess was about to give birth to divinely beautiful twins called Freda and Freddo—painlessly and without blood or slime. "You've probably seen those big white chalk horses on hillsides—installation art from the Bronze Age."

"When was the Bronze Age?" asked Granny.

"About two to four thousand years ago," said Jess's mum. "You'd have loved it. There was a large amount of gratuitous violence."

"Oh, lovely, dear!" said Granny. "I love those archeology

programs on the TV. Especially when they find those skulls that have been bashed in with a heavy object."

Jess sometimes thought that, in a previous existence, her granny might have been a ruthlessly brutal warlord.

"There's a figure I want you to see," said Mum. "It's in Dorset, on the hillside, cut out in the chalk. But it's not a horse."

Thank God, thought Jess. She had never really got into that whole horsy thing. She could imagine Flora galloping along a beach, her hair streaming in the wind like a shampoo ad, but Jess was sure that if she ever tried to meddle with horses she'd find herself upside down in a hedge, with her bra straps wrapped round a bird's nest.

If they were going to have to look at some of that Celtic chalk art stuff on a hillside, Jess would prefer it to be a fluffy kitten or cute puppy with a shiny wet nose.

"OK, here we are," said Mum, giggling rather foolishly as she pulled off the road and into a car park. "Don't look yet— just get out of the car and keep your eyes down on the ground." They piled out and kept their eyes down. Jess hoped her mum wouldn't go in for this *surprise surprise* thing too often. It seemed ever so slightly infantile.

"Right!" said Jess's mum. "Now look across the valley— over there."

"Oh my God!" Jess almost died with embarrassment. Across the valley, on the opposite hillside, and cut into the chalk like the white horse, was the gigantic figure of a naked man. No detail was missing, not even his private parts. In fact it would be true to say that no parts have ever been less private.

* 10 *

"Oh my God!" shrieked Jess. "Mum! How totally gross! What did you want to show us that for? It's like rank old porno!"

"OK," chuckled Jess's mum. "He is a bit overendowed in the lunchbox department."

"The lunchbox department!" cried Jess in disbelief, cringing. "Don't say that! Don't even go there!" Granny was screwing up her eyes and peering intently at the figure.

"It seems to me, dear," she said, "that his head is much smaller than his whatyamacallit."

"Well, that's men for you," said Jess's mum. "Tiny brains, obviously. He's a sort of fertility god. They did think he was thousands of years old, but now they reckon he only dates from maybe a couple of hundred years ago."

"These fertility figures!" said Jess. "Always lying about

44

their age. Trying to get into the history books. Like me trying to get into an eighteen-and-over film—which, incidentally, I would never dream of doing."

"Well, that was the Cerne Abbas Giant," said her mum as they piled back into the car. "And now we'll find a sweet little tea shop for lunch." It was the first sensible thing she'd said all morning.

The sweet little tea shop proved to be just moments away, in the village. Jess devoured a massive chunk of cheese and potato pie. Her next challenge was to control her burps as her half-pint of Coke jostled up unpleasantly against her massive high-fat lunch, which had been the size of a small but delicious child.

The waiter was a really cool guy, plump and with black curly hair and long dark eyelashes. When he brought the pudding menu, Mum looked up and gave him a cheeky grin.

"Has anyone ever said you look just like Tony Curtis in *Some Like It Hot*?" she asked. The guy shrugged, shook his head, and gave a doubtful smile.

"Most people say I look like a three-toed sloth," he said.

"Oh, sloths are so cute!" said Jess's mum, with a ghastly skittish laugh. "I suppose we all have animal look-alikes. When Jess was a baby we used to call her duckling because of her little turned-up beak."

Everybody at the table, in fact everybody in the café—possibly everybody in the whole world—turned to look at Jess for a split second. It was the worst moment in her life since the incident with the minestrone soup bra inserts. She glared back at her mother through a bright red fog of blushing, trying not to look too much like a duck.

45

"And what's your animal look-alike, Mum?" she hissed. "A skunk?"

"I'd like a tiny piece of apple pie with cream, please," said Granny, skillfully distracting attention away to the menu. "What about you, Jess? Some sticky toffee pudding?"

Jess didn't want a pudding. Her tummy was already hurting a bit. It would put rather a damper on the holiday if she was to explode before the end of the first day.

Dear Fred, thought Jess (she would get it down on paper later), *my mum has become completely deranged—forcing Bronze Age pornography on us, flirting with a waiter young enough to be her own son, and humiliating me in public. This holiday just gets better and better.*

"We're booked into a B and B in this village," said Mum, who had also passed on the pudding. "It's called The Lilacs. I think I'll just go and see if our rooms are ready, if you'll excuse me."

"I'll come with you," said Jess grimly. She had to get her mum on her own and give her a severe talking-to. Granny was quite happy to wait for them at the café with a slice of apple pie and a cup of tea. Jess and Mum set off down the village street.

"Now listen, Mum!" said Jess. "Promise me there won't be any more gigantic naked men on this trip! And do try and keep your hands off the waiters!"

"Oh, come on!" said Mum, grinning. "Give me a break! I've had such a dull old year in the library. I know I'm being a bit over the top, but I feel positively carefree for the first time in ages. The clouds! The sky! The medieval churches! I'm like a kid that's been let out of school!"

46

Bizarre. Usually it was Jess who was misbehaving and her mum laying down the law.

"Embarrass the hell out of me in public, then, why don't you?" said Jess. "Get drunk tonight and rip all your clothes off. Go for it."

"All right then, I'll try to behave," said Mum, as they arrived at The Lilacs. "But I might just go berserk again if I see something beautiful."

In front of the B and B there were very tall wrought-iron double gates, with pillars on both sides and stone balls on top.

"What a fabulous gate!" said Mum. "What a wonderful path!"

She was completely off her head. Any minute now she would start kissing the tarmac.

The door was opened by a tall thin man with a gray goatee. Mum introduced herself and immediately started to compliment him on the garden.

"What a marvelous gate!" she gushed. "And you've got the most wonderful pair of stone balls!"

"Could I have that in writing?" quipped the elderly gent, evidently game for a bit of mature flirtation. The two grown-ups joined in a peal of obscene laughter, whilst Jess gazed in torment at the flagstones in the porch and, not for the first time, wished she was in Timbuktu.

However, the B and B was really nice, with beautiful high-ceilinged rooms painted gray and yellow and blue. Jess's room overlooked a stream, and while Mum went back to get the car and fetch Granny, Jess lay on her bed and switched on her mobile.

There were two messages! One from Fred and another one from Dad. She read Fred's first. I'VE DECIDED TO LOOK FOR WORK. WILL SAVE UP TO GIVE YOU MASSIVE TREAT WHEN YOU GET BACK.

Was this boy divine or not? Hastily Jess sent a text in reply, briefly describing the horrors of the trip so far and promising to elope with him the moment she got home.

Dad's message was typically eccentric. DID YOU GET MY TEXT YESTERDAY? LOOKING FORWARD HUGELY TO WELCOMING YOU TO MY HUMBLE ABODE. HAVE ORDERED A CARTLOAD OF CAT FOOD AND A FLEA-COLLAR. Jess replied, CAN'T WAIT TO SCRATCH YOUR FURNITURE AND CATCH ALL YOUR DELICIOUS RATS.

Although she was still missing Fred like crazy, Jess was looking forward to seeing her dad again. He had such a surreal sense of humor. Unlike her mum. How on earth had her parents ever got together? It was a mystery. Maybe Jess would challenge him on the subject. Yes, she would back him into a corner and interrogate him, bigtime.

Later that afternoon another message came from Fred. GOT A FAB JOB! FOR A CATERER. AS WAITER. DOING A POSH WEDDING TOMORROW, LET'S HOPE LOTS OF TIPS. LOVE, FRED. Jess was pleased for him, of course. But part of her wished he hadn't managed to get a job quite so easily. She wouldn't have minded if he'd spent the whole time lying on his sofa and watching TV. In fact, she'd have preferred it.

ANY BEAUTIFUL GIRLS WORKING THERE? she texted back. NOT THAT I CARE, OF COURSE.

Fred's reply came back right away.

ALL GIRLS. KIND OF LOW–CALORIE SUGABABES. What the hell did he mean by that? Terror seized Jess's soul. She was sure that by tomorrow night one of the low-calorie Sugababes would have struck. Fred had a terrible sweet tooth. This was the beginning of the end.

* 11 *

*J*ess went down to breakfast, following a delicious smell of bacon. However, she was slightly alarmed to see that Granny had brought Grandpa's ashes down to the dining room with her. His urn was right there on the table, between the salt and pepper. Jess was speechless, and tried to concentrate on her cornflakes.

"When I was about your age," said Mum, out of the blue, "I had a crush on somebody."

"For goodness' sake, Mum!" said Jess. "Keep these embarrassing confessions to yourself."

"I'm only mentioning it," her mum went on, "because it's to do with the place we're going to today."

"Who was it?" asked Jess. "One of those sixties rock stars? A crinkly old Rolling Stone?"

"No," said her mum. "It was a bit unusual, I suppose—

because he'd been dead for forty years. And his name," she went on, with the shy but triumphant air of one confessing to a relationship with some kind of major celeb, "was Lawrence of Arabia."

"Who?" asked Jess. She had sort of heard of him, but she wasn't sure how.

"There was that epic movie about him in the 1960s," said Mum. "They reissued it a couple of years ago. He was a great hero in Arabia, during the First World War. Then after the war, he came back and lived as a recluse in a tiny cottage tucked away in a corner of Dorset."

Jess stopped listening. All she cared about was the next text from Fred. She couldn't help torturing herself with the thought of him at that wedding, surrounded by low-calorie Sugababes. The fact that he had described them as Sugababes had started to annoy her. Couldn't he have said "a pack of dogs" or "a horde of hideous heifers" just to reassure her—even if it wasn't true?

"I remember you had a poster of Lawrence of Arabia, pinned up on your wall," said Granny.

"Did I?" said Mum, sounding rather embarrassed. "Maybe. I don't remember."

"Did you dream about marrying him, even though he was dead?" asked Jess.

"No, I didn't fantasize about being married to him," said Mum. "I think I wanted to *be* Lawrence of Arabia."

"From what I heard," said Granny, "he wasn't the marrying kind." And she gave a kind of obscene wink.

"What do you mean, Granny?" asked Jess. "Do you mean he was gay?"

"It wasn't done, in those days, dear," said Granny. "People used to keep very quiet about such things. There were men who never married, that's all. They used to be called confirmed bachelors."

"Personally I think he was just celibate," said Mum. "But he may have been gay. Some people think so. Now, of course, it's fine. Statistically, one in ten people is gay. Although that figure has been disputed." This was turning into a lecture on sexual politics. Jess's mind began to wander back to the wretched Sugababes.

"In fact," Mum went on, "some people you know quite well might turn out to be gay." Jess's attention was suddenly right back in the here and now.

"Mum! Don't tell me you're a lesbian! I mean, I love lesbians, they're cool, I just don't like life-changing surprises over breakfast!"

"No, no, of course not!" said Mum. "Don't be silly. Anyway, enough of that." Mum whipped her napkin off her knee and wiped her mouth. She went off to pay the guesthouse bill, and soon they were on the road again, heading for Lawrence of Arabia's cottage.

Jess couldn't concentrate on Lawrence of Arabia. She could feel herself sinking into a horrific but somehow compulsive fantasy about Fred being a waiter with three gorgeous girls all in short black skirts competing for his attention.

In Jess's imagination, there was a blonde called Grace, who would appeal to his higher nature. Jess was sure there would also be a dark girl with sultry lips called Selina. She would appeal to his baser instincts. And worst of all, there would be a redhead called Charlie—such a sassy name for a girl—who was not particularly good-looking but had the most magnetic personality and the funniest gags. It was Charlie Jess was most afraid of.

"He died a very tragic death." Her mum broke into the fantasy with yet another of her depressing asides. "Is it next left, Granny?"

"No, next but one," said Granny, navigating with loveable excitement. "By a phone box, according to the map. How did he die, dear? I can't remember."

"He fell into a bowl of parsnip soup and was drowned," suggested Jess.

"No," said Mum, putting on a pious air. "It was tragic. He used to ride about on a motorbike. He swerved to avoid two errand boys, and went off the road and crashed. He never regained consciousness. I think he was in hospital for a few days, sort of hanging on. But he died."

"I wonder if he had one of those out-of-the-body experiences," mused Granny. "You read so much about them. A lot of people have had them. They're lying on their hospital bed, and then suddenly they're floating up by the ceiling and they hear a voice say—turn right by that chip shop, dear—'Your time has not yet come.'

"Still," Granny went on, "at least he didn't have a wife and family, so there wasn't that immediate sort of family loss."

"The nation grieved," said Jess's mum, in a pompous tone of voice, as if she was in the pulpit of a cathedral somewhere. "And one might say the fact that he wasn't married with children was even more tragic." She sighed, as if she would have given anything to bear a glamorous son for Lawrence of Arabia, rather than a slightly stout and bad-tempered daughter for Tim Jordan.

Soon they arrived at Clouds Hill, and Jess clambered stoutly and bad-temperedly out of the car. This was a remote spot. Wind tossed the grass and leaves about in a rather haunted way. Jess's mum looked up at the clouds, and a strange, dreamlike expression came over her face.

"Clouds Hill . . . I've wanted to come here for years and years, you've no idea," she murmured, and walked off to the entrance place.

Clouds Hill was a weird, tiny house. There was no electricity. It was dark indoors, and plain, and it smelt peculiar.

"I do think he might have got himself a decent sofa," said Granny. "I don't like the look of those chairs. They look so uncomfortable. It gives me backache just to look at them."

"To think that he actually sat there!" said Jess's mum, staring in fascination at the chair upon which Lawrence of Arabia's charismatic buttocks had reposed. "I was crazy about him when I was young. It would have been much healthier if I'd had a proper boyfriend—one my own age."

Wow, thought Jess, *is Mum fishing? Does she maybe have a hunch that Fred and I are an Item?* It would be so, so cool if Mum knew about Fred and approved and everything. It was just that Mum had often been kind of hard on men, and Jess hadn't quite managed to pluck up her courage and mention the subject. But was this her chance?

Jess's heart started to beat impossibly fast. She must say something. She knew Fred wanted her to tell her mum about him.

"As a matter of fact," said Jess, in a casual, airy kind of

way, "I've got a proper boyfriend—somebody my own age."

Mum whirled round, her face transformed in an instant. Her blissful yearning for the spirit of Lawrence of Arabia was replaced by a wide-eyed alarm and terror. As if she'd suddenly seen a snake in a flower bed.

"What?" she spat. "What's all this? What on earth are you talking about?"

Oh my God, thought Jess, *I've blown it.* In an instant the skittish holiday Mum had gone, and the anxious, disapproving old bat of normal everyday life was back in charge. Jess would have to blag her way out of this one.

"Yeah," she went on, "haven't I mentioned him? His name's Siegfried de Montenegro and his family made a million out of marzipan. They live in a castle on a hill in Transylvania. We're planning a December wedding and I'm going to have a troupe of vampires-in-honor, all in pink and white."

Mum's face cleared. She shook her head in some kind of disbelief, as if Jess had just made a very tasteless joke, and went back to ogling Lawrence of Arabia's furniture. Phew! That had been a dodgy moment and no mistake.

Jess felt sad. If only her mum had said, "What, Fred? Perfect choice—I adore the lad. He can come round anytime and I'll make some jam tarts specially." But it didn't seem as if she would be able to say that, ever. Jess and Fred would have to remain a secret for years and years and years. Till they were middle-aged—twenty-five, at least.

Jess completely switched off from her surroundings. She was oblivious to Clouds Hill. She was wondering what was going on at that wedding where Fred was being a waiter.

* 12 *

by J.J.

*I*n Jess's imagination, there was a huge marquee on
a lawn, and a lot of smartly dressed people were
milling about under some massive oak trees. Fred,
dressed in a black suit and wearing a cute little bow tie, was
pouring out champagne.

"Can I top you up?" he asked a ravishing young woman in
a powder blue two-piece and a massive hat adorned with
ostrich feathers. Somehow it sounded faintly obscene, as if
topping her up might involve Fred escorting her behind the
marquee and sticking his tongue down her throat.

"Well, *hello!*" said the young woman in a swoopy sort of
voice. She was called, er—Jemima. Jemima Featherstone-
FFyffe. "I wasn't thinking of having any more champagne,"
breathed Jemima, "but since it's you—why not? Tell me,
what do you do when you're not being a waiter?"

"Oh, I write screenplays," said Fred airily. "I'm working on one about a rabbit who saves the world."

"Wow! That sounds fabulous!" exclaimed Jemima F-FF. Somehow she had got rid of her powder blue suit and was wearing a glittering swimsuit and moonstone earrings that looked like two divine dewdrops hanging from her perfect ears. "You must meet my father, he's a film director. Come with me. . . ." And she clasped Fred's elbow and steered him away through the crowds.

"Tell me," Jemima whispered to Fred, "please don't think I'm being too forward, but—do you have a girlfriend? Are you going out with one of those waitresses?" She cast a glance at Charlie, Selina, and Grace, who were handing out exquisite little pastries whilst also glaring in Fred's direction, because each of them had been secretly planning to seduce him herself.

"Oh no," said Fred. "I did have a sort of girlfriend, but it wasn't really a big thing, you know, and besides . . . she's gone off for the whole summer with her tiresome family."

"How could she leave you unattended for a split second?" inquired Jemima, who had turned into a kind of South Sea Island Goddess wearing only high-heeled shoes and a bikini made of fig leaves.

"I'm afraid she is rather careless that way," said Fred, shrugging. And they dissolved into a kind of swamp of snogging behind a potted palm. All the wedding guests peeped discreetly at them, murmuring to one another, "Isn't it fabulous? Jemima seems to be getting off with that cute waiter. Poor girl, she really deserves cheering up after that awful incident with Don and the white water rafting."

Back in the real world, Jess was in the Lawrence of Arabia bookshop. There were lots of books about him. They all had photos of him on their dust jackets. His face was long and fair and handsome, but somehow haunted and a bit weird. You just knew he was the sort of guy who would never smile for photographs.

"I tell you what," said Granny. "He's the spitting image of your father, dear."

Jess looked closely at the photos and thought for a bit.

"Well, I suppose he does look a bit like Dad, in a way," she said. Lawrence of Arabia had the same kind of long floppy hair. It fell down on each side of his brow.

"Dad is a lot taller than Lawrence was," said Jess's mum. She made it sound as if this was a mistake on Daddy's part. If he had any tact he wouldn't have done all that growing, but remained glamorously short.

"When are we going to see Dad, Mum?" asked Jess. "I can't wait to see him again!" And just at the very moment when, for a split second, Jess had got excited about something on this history tour, she felt her mobile vibrate in her pocket. A message from Fred!

"Early next week," said her mum. "We'll be down in St. Ives by then."

"Great! Cool! Well, I'm going to get some fresh air— excuse me," said Jess, desperate to be alone with her text. She strolled outdoors and whipped out her mobile. She had been so longing to hear from him. But she hadn't wanted to text him all the time, all needy and nerdy.

DISASTER, it said, MANAGED TO DROP A BIG DISH OF CRÈME CARAMEL ALL DOWN CHARLOTTE'S CLEAVAGE.

Oh no! It was even worse than Jess's tortured fantasy. She didn't even know who Charlotte was, but whether she was one of the Sugababe waitresses, or a seductive wedding guest like Jemima, Fred had already got on such close terms with her cleavage that lurve and marriage must surely follow.

Jess didn't answer Fred's text right away, as she usually did. She was too horrified. She didn't trust herself. She was afraid she might say something really ferocious. On the other hand, boy, did she want to say something ferocious!

Instead she resorted to prayer. Sometimes things got so feverish you just had to hope there was some lovable old guy in the sky with a long white beard and twinkly, compassionate eyes, like Gandalf.

Dear Lord, thought Jess fervently, *I know you disapprove of cleavages, and I'm sorry that, at certain moments in the past, I have tried to improve mine with the aid of minestrone soup bra inserts. Forgive me, Lord, and—this is just a suggestion—why don't we make it anticleavage week? You could start by removing Charlotte's during the night and replacing it with an endless dreary flatness, covered with matted red fur.*

13

fter visiting Clouds Hill, they drove off to a town called Dorchester. Mum had booked them into a little B and B in a side street. Mum and Granny had a twin-bedded room at the front, and Jess had a tiny room at the back with a fabulous view of a brick wall. Somehow this seemed to reflect her mood.

Mum made a cup of tea in her room, and Jess sat on Granny's bed. There was a game show on the TV, but Jess was hardly listening. Privately, she was rehearsing ferocious texts to Fred— messages so furious she would never, ever send them.

WHY DON'T YOU JUST DIVE STRAIGHT INTO HER CLEAVAGE? DON'T HESITATE ON MY ACCOUNT . . . I COULD POINT OUT THAT "CHARLOTTE" RHYMES WITH "HARLOT" BUT PERHAPS IT'S BETTER IF I JUST SAY GOODBYE. . . .

DID YOU LICK IT OFF? BET YOU WANTED TO. . . . IS CHAR-

LOTTE PRETTIER THAN ME? WELL, SO IS 90% OF THE FEMALE
POPULATION. . . . GO FOR IT, FRED PARSONS. WHY NOT? AF-
TER ALL, I HAVE BEEN AWAY A WHOLE TWO DAYS.

After they'd unpacked their bags, there was an hour before
supper.

"I'm just going for a walk around town," said Jess. She felt
so stressed out, she couldn't just sit still in her room.

Within minutes of leaving the B and B, Jess found a branch
of the Body Shop. She went in, grabbed a few testers and
sprayed herself wildly all over: coconut, vanilla, melon. . . .
Never had aromatherapy been more desperately needed.

Although why did Body Shop cosmetics have to be so inti-
mately related to food? Food meant catering, and catering
meant Fred being a waiter and smothering sexy girls with
delicious puddings. Melon, vanilla, coconut—Jess doubted if
she'd ever be able to enjoy any of them again. Not now that
dessert had started to feature in Fred's love life.

"Are you OK?" asked the salesgirl. *No,* thought Jess, *my heart
is broken.* But she smiled politely and said, "Yes, thanks."

Then she investigated approximately one thousand lip
glosses before selecting the very first one she had tried.
Would this lip gloss win back Fred's fickle heart? Jess glared
moodily at herself in a mirror. No wonder Fred couldn't stay
faithful to her for more than a split second. With her slightly
plump cheeks and tiny eyes, she looked like some kind of
crazed hamster.

She paid for the lip gloss and left. A few yards further
along, Jess found a stationery shop. Yessss! She would buy
some elegant, seductive paper and deluge Fred with witty,
scintillating, passionate letters. It might not be quite as

mesmerizing as Charlotte's cleavage covered with pudding, but it was Jess's only hope.

Jess bought some postcards too. She bought some Marilyn Monroe and Humphrey Bogart ones for her dad, who worshipped old movie stars. And she bought some photos of a dull old church for Fred. She wasn't going to send him an image of the divine Marilyn—it might make him even more disappointed with her own rather low-key physical assets.

She also bought some terribly charismatic sage green writing paper, raced back to the B and B, and started to write. First she wrote a card to Dad, describing Mum's ludicrous crush on Lawrence of Arabia. Then she texted her dad. DAD—I JUST WROTE YOU A POSTCARD. HOPE YOU'RE IMPRESSED! I'M SENDING YOU THIS TEXT JUST IN CASE I NEVER GET AROUND TO POSTING IT. THERE'S SOMETHING I NEED TO KNOW. HOW IMPORTANT ARE CLEAVAGES? IF A GUY IS FACED WITH A REAL HUMDINGER, CAN HE LOOK AWAY AND WISH HE WAS WITH HIS FLAT-CHESTED GIRLFRIEND? LOVE, JESS.

That was her dad sorted. Now it was time for her letter to Fred. She would not mention Charlotte. She would ignore the whole thing.

Dear Fred,
     Today we visited Lawrence of Arabia's cottage. Terribly atmospheric. Judging by the photos he looks quite like my dad. I can't wait to see Dad again. I wish you could meet him, though he is rather childish. I know I've told you about how weird and mysterious he is, but there's nothing like meeting people face to face, is there? He's

certainly a lot more entertaining than my mum.
Her obsession with history is ruining my life.
     Tomorrow we shall visit the scene of King
Arthur's brave stand against the gerbils, plus a
fascinating chapel where St. Horace had a vision
of a pork pie with wings in the year 1238. It was
a sign that the famine would shortly end.
Speaking of food, it's time for supper. Judging by
my massive hips, I should try and confine myself
to a single lettuce leaf. But knowing me I shall
give in to temptation and swallow a whole live cow.

She had tried very hard to write a lively, lighthearted letter.
But Jess was still sunk in a horrible black mood. She planned
to murder Fred a million different ways. Or possibly murder
the low-calorie Sugababes by hurling them into hot tea and
stirring violently with a giant, cruel spoon.

Jess went out, bought some stamps, and posted her letter to
Fred and her card to her dad. Then she went back to the hotel
and watched *The Simpsons* on TV until it was time for supper.

At suppertime they went out to an Italian restaurant. Jess
devoured her pasta with grim determination. She still hadn't
replied to Fred's text message about Charlotte's cleavage.
She hoped he was in agony, waiting. But on the other hand,
he just might be staring into Charlotte's eyes and showering
her with his divine jokes and clever compliments. And if this
was the scenario, Jess was definitely never going to speak to
him again.

"Hah!" she would sneer glamorously at him, when eventually
they met again. "So you've come crawling back, have you? Has

the wonderful Charlotte told you to push off? Or have you tired of her magnificent, pudding-stained cleavage?"

"Forgive me!" gasped Fred, throwing himself facedown on the carpet—no, wait, that wasn't public enough. The park. Yes! The bandstand! With a huge crowd watching. "I love only you! Charlotte forced me to throw puddings at her! I never enjoyed it for a moment! And I never touched her, except with wet wipes!"

"Crawl in the dust, you faithless viper!" spat Jess. "For I shall never speak to you again, no, not for a hundred years." She was beginning to sound a bit like the Bible. She quite liked it. She turned on her heel and stalked off, leaving Fred groveling.

"And another thing!" She turned back to him. "Eat dirt, Fred Parsons! No matter how hard you beg, you shall never receive another glance or word from me!"

Fred kind of frothed at the mouth like a dog who has swallowed something a bit poisonous, and scrabbled in the dirt. Jess tossed a last stony, scornful glance at him, curled her lip in contempt, and turned her back on him. A murmur of pity and horror ran through the watching millions—for this scene was being beamed around the world on satellite TV.

And then suddenly, back in the real world, her phone buzzed in her bag.

"What's that, dear?" said Granny in alarm. "Is it one of your e-mails?"

"Text messages, Granny," said Jess, grabbing her phone. "It'll just be Flora."

"You should switch your phone off in restaurants," said Mum, never one to miss the chance of a moan.

"Yeah, yeah—in a minute," said Jess, trying to look cool and collected as Fred's message flashed up.

WHAT THE HELL'S GOING ON? WHY SO SILENT? ARE YOU FLIRTING WITH SOME DUMB LIFEGUARD CALLED GARETH?

Hastily she composed what she hoped would be a devastating retort.

HOW'S CHARLOTTE'S CLEAVAGE THIS EVENING? STILL MESMERIZING?

She pressed the SEND button with a sort of bitter panache. How dare he be jealous of her, when she had done nothing but think about him for three whole days, solid? Whilst he frolicked with girls and noticed their cleavages, the bastard!

"I told you to switch the blasted thing off now, Jess!" said Mum, getting quite ratty.

"OK, OK, Mum, no need for stress! I am switching it off," said Jess.

Even as she spoke, a message came back.

CHARLOTTE IS FIFTY AND OUR BOSS, DUMBO. HER CLEAVAGE IS ABOUT AS APPEALING AS A CREVASSE IN ANTARCTICA.

Huge, huge relief swept through Jess. Dear, darling Fred! She had been so stupid. She had wasted the whole day being jealous completely without any reason. How could she apologize in a way which would be graceful and yet, somehow, seductively hilarious?

Whilst she was racking her brains, another message arrived. Eagerly Jess peered at the tiny screen. What message was adorable Fred sending her now? A declaration of undying love?—Oh no! Jess's blood ran cold with horror.

IT'S ROSIE YOU REALLY OUGHT TO WORRY ABOUT. . . .

65

hen she got back to the B and B, Jess was alone at last in her own little room. But, disaster! She was right out of credit on her mobile. She couldn't send Fred a text giving him hell about that Rosie gag. If it was a gag. Being apart like this really sucked.

All night Jess tossed and turned. She hardly managed to sleep at all, and when she did, Fred was misbehaving in her dreams with whole hockey teams. Eventually dawn came, and Jess fell into a deep sleep. And then Mum knocked on her door and she had to drag herself up because it was time for breakfast, even though it still felt like the middle of the night.

Jess slouched down to the dining room like a zombie out of one of those old black-and-white movies. She was pretty black and white, herself. Her mood was dark and her face was pale and ghastly. She had meant to wake up early and rush out and buy some more credit for her phone, but of course she had failed dismally.

"Jess," said Granny, "you look awful! What's wrong?"

"Couldn't sleep," said Jess, sitting down.

"Never mind, dear," said Granny, patting her hand. "Have some bacon and eggs. That'll soon put you right."

Granny squeezed her hand and stroked her hair. It was sweet of her, but kind of irritating as well. Jess declined the bacon and eggs. For the first time on the whole trip, she didn't feel very hungry. She was sure bacon and eggs would taste of dust and ashes.

Speaking of dust and ashes, thank goodness Granny had left Grandpa's urn upstairs this time. One does not want to see the mortal remains of one's grandparent gracing the breakfast table.

"Just toast will do today," Jess said, sadly.

"Right," said Jess's mum, pouring out the tea with a secret smile which Jess just knew had something to do with history. Her heart would've sunk if it hadn't already been reposing on the inky depths of the ocean floor. "Today's a real highlight of our trip," Mum went on. "We're going to see somebody's grave."

Oh, yippee, thought Jess. *Terrific. A grave. How life-enhancing. How delightful. I might have known it.*

"A grave?" said Granny, brightening visibly. "Whose?"

"Thomas Hardy's," said Jess's mum with an air of triumph. "Now, Jess, do you know anything about him?"

Jess was silent. Even if she had known all there was to know about Thomas Hardy, she wouldn't have said a word. Even if she had babysat for him and eaten his toast and read his private letters.

"Haven't a clue," she croaked. "Pass the marmalade, please, Granny. Anyone got a headache pill?" Perhaps if her mum thought she was ill, she would hold back on the history. Vain hope.

"Thomas Hardy wrote a lot of novels, all set down here in Dorset," said Mum, with ridiculous excitement, as if she'd just found a winning lottery ticket. "He had quite a sad life, really," Mum went on. *So what else is new,* thought Jess. Everyone on this trip so far had had a tragic life. And it looked as if Jess's was going to be no exception.

"He married a woman called Emma, but he was so busy that he sort of took her for granted, and then suddenly she died, and he was heartbroken. He felt so guilty that he hadn't appreciated her enough, and he wrote loads of love-poems to her after her death."

Jess was quite struck with this idea. She made plans to die immediately, so that Fred would be convulsed with guilt and visit her tomb daily with a freshly written sonnet. And he would neglect his personal appearance, of course, even more than usual. Dramatically. Mushrooms would grow out of his ears. No girl would ever look at him again. And of course, he would never look at another girl. He would even avert his eyes from MTV.

"Anyway," said Mum, "when he died, he'd left instructions that his heart was to be removed and buried in his first wife's grave."

"Gross!" screamed Jess.

"What did they do with the rest of him?" asked Granny.

"The rest of him was buried in Westminster Abbey. In Poets' Corner."

"How bizarre," said Jess.

"Did you say his *first* wife's grave?" asked Granny, with a Miss Marple–like pounce. She did sometimes resemble the elderly TV detective.

"Oh yes. He did eventually marry again."

"What, he married again, but he asked for his heart to be buried with his first wife?" said Jess.

"Yes. Exactly."

"Weird," said Jess. What sort of second wife would put up with that kind of thing? If Fred ever told her he wanted his heart to be buried with a previous girlfriend, Jess would personally eat it with barbecue sauce and fries.

"Oh, look!" said Granny. "The sun's just come out! It's going to be another lovely day!"

Huh! Granny! What did she know? *Nothing.*

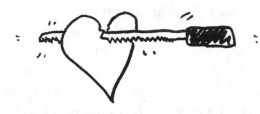

"It's not far to Hardy's grave!" trilled Jess's mum excitedly, backing the car out of the parking space with slightly too much panache. As if Jess cared. Hardy's grave could be at the other end of the Zarg galaxy, and she wouldn't have turned a hair.

She had begged Mum to let her rush to the nearest shop and buy some more credit for her phone, but Mum had been adamant that they must have an early start, and that Jess was spending far too much time on the wretched thing, anyway.

"Steady on, Madeleine!" said Granny. "You nearly hit that wall!"

"Don't nag, Mum," said Jess's mum. "You know I'm the safest driver in the whole country, so just give me a break."

Hey! Maybe Mum and Granny were finding it hard, sharing a room. Maybe they'd had a blazing row, and maybe

Mum had gone off in a sulk, locked herself in the bathroom, and scrawled *Mum is a loser* on the mirror, in soap. Mum still called Granny Mum sometimes. It was a little strange imagining Mum as a sulking teenager. But then, Jess supposed even Granny must have been a sulking teenager once.

Jess smiled to herself at the thought. The smile felt strange on her face. She realized she hadn't done any of that smiling or laughing business for days.

"At least it's not far," said Mum. "Just a few miles to the churchyard."

Jess was annoyed that it wasn't very far. She would gladly have stayed slumped in the back of the car all day, watching listlessly as the countryside rolled past—preferably a countryside of horrid precipices, rocks, ravens, and pine trees struck by lightning.

Alas, this kind of countryside was not typical of the South West of England, and she had to put up with sunlit meadows, cute cuddly hills, and occasional glimpses of twinkling sea.

Jess was longing to get to the sea and stay there. Mum had said they would stay several days by the sea once they'd got down to Cornwall. When they arrived anywhere with a beach, Jess was planning to go out and sit and stare at the waves. She just hoped the beach would be deserted. It would be awful to have to share her mood of tragic despair with hordes of screaming kids smearing themselves with ice cream.

Somehow this thought led to Fred. How ironic that the best person on the planet had been left behind. If only he'd been with them, she was sure that Thomas Hardy's heart would have acquired a hilarious glamour. It would be top of the list of wacky tourist attractions. Fred would have thought of a hundred even more weird things to do with one's body after death. Being separated from him made the whole planet seem poisoned and pointless.

"Here we are!" cried Mum gaily, as they drove down a shady lane towards a tiny church deeply veiled in trees. The last place on earth where you could buy credit for a mobile phone.

"This is where we'll see his grave!" said Mum with ghoulish rapture. *Jackpot*, thought Jess.

"His ashes were buried in Westminster Abbey," said Granny, consulting the guidebook. "They must have got the heart out before he was cremated, then. I wonder who does that sort of thing?" Granny had an almost indecent interest in such matters. For a moment Jess was afraid she might get the urn out of the car boot, and take Grandpa's ashes to visit Thomas Hardy's heart.

However, she refrained, thank goodness, so it was only the living members of the party who went through the little gate into the tiny churchyard. Jess saw the grave immediately, on the left of the path. THOMAS HARDY, it said.

"Here it is!" she said. She wanted to get this over as soon as possible and get back to daydreaming in the back of the car.

"Oh no, love, that's not it," said her mum.

"But it says *Thomas Hardy*."

"That's not him. The dates are too early. That's another Thomas Hardy. I think that must be his father—or possibly grandfather. Let me work out the dates. . . ." There were several tombs all in a row, and each one said Thomas Hardy on it.

Jess was gutted. She hadn't even managed to find the correct Thomas Hardy. Why did there have to be so many of them? There seemed to be a whole epidemic. Wasn't it a little bit unimaginative of his parents to call him Thomas, knowing there were so many Thomas Hardys in the family history? Why hadn't they called him Leonardo or Oliver? Or Dave?

"Here's the one!" said Granny. "It says about his heart being buried here. In his first wife's grave, you know—Emma Lavinia Gifford."

"Here's a poem he wrote to the memory of Emma," said Jess's mum, getting a book out of her pocket and opening it at a page marked by a bus ticket. She started to read, in a silly sort of breathless, yearning voice:

"*I stand here in the rain,*
With its smite upon her stone,
And the grasses that have grown . . ."

"Stop! Mum!" said Jess. "Don't read poems out in public! Weird!"

"Don't be silly, Jess," said her mum. "There's nobody about." And she instantly resumed. Jess shook her head in disbelief, and caught Granny's eye.

Granny leaned towards Jess and whispered, "Just let her have her way, dear. She always was incurably romantic."

The thought of her mother as an incurable romantic was about as bizarre as the thought of her granny as a champion tennis player. Jess looked up at the trees and deliberately didn't listen to the poem. She was wishing she was a bird.

And if I was a bird, she thought, *I'd fly straight back home and find Fred, and if he was with Rosie I'd crap on her head, obviously, and she'd run off. And then I'd perch on Fred's shoulder forever, and roost inside his vest, and never leave him.*

This fantasy was somehow quite comforting, and after

they'd seen the inside of the church, they got back into the car, so today's indigestible dose of history seemed to be safely over. Jess wrote a Humphrey Bogart postcard to Flora.

Dear Flo. Having a totally dire holiday. Mum is dragging me round endless graveyards reading out awful poems in a sad nerdy voice. My granny is carting the ashes of my grandpa around with her. And Fred is apparently falling for somebody called Rosie. Have fun—somebody's got to. Love, Jess.

Maybe she should send another card to Dad.

Hi, Dad! Thomas Hardy was cut up and buried in two separate places! Sick or what? Have you decided where you want to be buried? Never die, though—I'll kill you if you do. This trip has been so depressing, only a cute puppy can cheer me up. See to it! Love, Jess

After she had finished both the cards and stuck the stamps on, Jess went back to the idea of herself as Fred's pet canary, and stayed there whilst her mum drove for ages, out of the county of Dorset and into Devon.

"You'll notice," said Mum, "that the lanes in Devon are very deep, and the soil is wonderfully red." Such an optimist. Jess was living in a dream world, and would hardly have noticed if Devon had been inhabited by dragons and the soil had been composed of chocolate cake.

74

16

Jess mess
bless cress
stress confess
success less

ventually they arrived at the town where Mum was
planning to stay the night. It was called Totnes. Jess
cheered up. It looked like the kind of fun, busy place
where mobile phone credit would be widely available.
What else mattered?

"I've always wanted to come here," Mum said, parking er-
ratically as usual, rather too close to a camper van. It seemed to
Jess that her mother always wanted to go everywhere. Maybe
she had not received the correct careers advice. Maybe she
should not have been a librarian, but a travel rep.

Although travel reps always had to wear such dismal
uniforms. Jess could not imagine her mum in a sky blue
polyester suit, crisp shirt, and idiotic cravat. Mind you,
Mum's usual clothes were in a weird class of their own.

Today she was wearing a pair of black loose trousers,

lightly scattered with stars (and, to be honest, tea stains), a Bob Marley T-shirt, and a cardigan knitted in Peru and showing native peoples involved in what looked like human sacrifice.

But strangely, everybody else in Totnes looked remarkably similar. This was certainly Mum's kind of place. Immediately after parking the car they found a tea shop, in response to Granny's plaintive plea: "I'm gasping for a cuppa!"

It was called Fat Lemon—a strange name for a tea shop, but somehow, Jess suspected, typical of Totnes. They had so far only walked down one street but had already seen three old hippies with beards and two middle-aged women wearing gypsyish skirts and head scarves adorned with sequins and fringes.

"They have over seventy varieties of tea!" exclaimed Granny, reading the menu. Seventy! This was somewhat excessive, surely.

"What poetic names!" said Mum. "*Emperor's Choice, Russian Caravan, Mountain Green* . . ." Oh no! She was doing that poetry-reading thing again.

Jess ordered hot chocolate and a fabulous cheesy vegetarian bake. She soon began to feel a bit more cheerful. She liked the Fat Lemon. It was a great name. Thomas Hardy's parents should have called him Fat Lemon instead of Thomas. Fat Lemon Hardy—he could have been a jazz trumpeter instead of a tortured and tragic writer.

"Feeling better, dear?" whispered Granny.

"Yes, thanks, Granny!" Jess squeezed Granny's withered old hand. It was like a bundle of twigs. Granny's eyes sometimes had a faraway, cloudy gray look which only old people's eyes seemed to have. As if they were looking into the next world, or something.

Jess was alarmed to feel tears gathering behind her face! Oh no! Curse this premenstrual tension! Hastily she switched into a different gear.

"What are we going to see tomorrow, Mum?" she asked. Her mum looked startled. It was the first time Jess had shown any interest at all in the trip.

"I want to take you to Berry Pomeroy Castle," said Mum. "They say it's the most haunted place in the country." At this point everybody in the tea room should have suddenly gone quiet, and a cloud should have covered the sun. But all the customers just went on noisily eating their vegetarian delicacies and arguing about herbs and crystals.

"Great!" said Jess. "I love haunted places! In fact, I want to be a ghost when I grow up."

"Don't worry, dear," whispered Granny with a cheery wink. "You will be."

In Totnes they were booked into a rickety old hotel in a fairly noisy part of town. Jess's room had a grandstand view: street life bustled away below, like a scene in a movie. But nobody in Totnes even faintly resembled Fred.

Now was her chance to go and buy more phone credit. But she decided to dash off another quick letter to Fred first, so she could catch the afternoon post.

Dearest Fred, she wrote, we are now in Totnes, hippy capital of the southwest. Here you can buy handmade shoes cunningly crafted from recycled loo rolls. My granny was elated by a café selling seventy different types of tea. But she just ordered the same old boring tea as usual.

My mum decided to splash out and be adventurous, so she ordered a quaint brew made from camel's droppings in remote Poshbeckistan. But then she decided she didn't really like it. That's my mum's life, summed up in a single tragic teatime.

Earlier we visited the tomb of a tragic guy called Tom who wrote tragic novels about tragic people. It was a blast. He had a pretty tragic life himself. He only realized he loved his wife after she died. So he left orders that after his death his heart must be cut out and buried with her. I can't decide whether this is unbearably moving or horrendously gross, but I demand the same tribute from you, or there will be trouble, big—time.

Anyway, it has given me the idea of writing my will. If I die first, I want to be stuffed. I want you to take my lifeless corpse out to a nightclub every Saturday. You can do this small thing for me, can't you? And for God's sake make sure they get my eyebrows right. Halfway between witty Manhattan journo and crazy Egyptian princess living in a garret in Paris.

I hope you are working hard and averting

your eyes from Charlotte's cleavage, however wrinkly. But if this Rosie character is taking my place in your heart, be advised that I shall personally cut out the aforementioned organ after your death. In fact, why wait for your death? I'll cut it out whilst you're still alive, stuff it with chicken livers, and toss it to the nearest wolves.

I'm in the mood now. I'm getting into my stride. I won't rest until the pair of you are charcuterie. It's not that I'm jealous or anything. But if Rosie really exists, tell her she can wave her ovaries goodbye. You can flirt with her all you like, you treacherous swine, but by God you won't breed with her as long as there's breath in my body. Hope you're well.

Love, Jess

ess popped Fred's letter in an envelope, sealed it, and pressed a passionate kiss on the seal. Unfortunately the Body Shop lip gloss left a telltale smear. Jess took the envelope to the bathroom and tried to wipe the lip gloss off. But it just smeared it about even worse.

In the end she decided to do the sensible thing and kissed the envelope all over. Now it just looked as if it had fallen onto the floor of the sorting office and been trodden on by a postman whose route included a swampy area inhabited by incontinent donkeys.

OK, that was fine. Now she would go out and post it. She picked up her personal stereo and mobile phone and walked out of the room. She walked up and down the incredibly steep old main street until she found a post box, where she hesitated for a moment. The next fingers to touch the letter would be Fred's. Her fingers kind of burned erotically as she let it go.

A few moments later she realized that the next person to touch the envelope would probably be a fat lady in the sorting office. Things are never quite as magical as one would hope.

Next she bought some credit for her mobile phone. At last communication could be restored between Jess and her beloved—well, all her beloveds, in fact. Her dad was certainly deeply beloved and Flora was the best friend in the world. First, though, Jess composed a text for Fred.

HOLIDAY GHASTLY TRUST YOU ARE ALSO IN AGONY. HAVE JUST POSTED YOU A LETTER. But when she tried to send it, she got the message FAILED. Oh no! There was no service here.

She was tempted to ring him from a pay phone, but she only had 20p with her—hardly enough for a cough. And anyway, he'd be working now—he worked every evening. His mobile would be switched off. And if he did pick up, he might be with Rosie.

It would be just awful to ring Fred if he was all polite and distant. Or even worse, if he said he couldn't talk and hung up on her. Possibly with mocking girlish laughter echoing in the background. It would be worse than not speaking to him at all.

Supper was in the hotel, because Granny was rather tired and couldn't face climbing up the hill to a restaurant. Jess ordered chicken, even though she had completely lost her appetite.

Jess's mum spent a lot of time talking about her alarm clock, and the fact that she couldn't get it to work. This was a bit of a relief, because it took care of the conversation. Jess was also glad that her mum didn't say anything weird and sad about men. Also, she had made an effort to look passable. She had changed into a black silk shirt and black crêpe trousers.

"You look really nice tonight, Mum," said Jess pointedly. Her mum looked surprised and a bit panicky. "Black suits you. You should wear silver earrings, though."

Jess's mum was very obviously not wearing silver. Instead she had on a pair of earrings shaped like palm trees made out of painted wood. This was a major style failure, though possibly acceptable in Totnes.

Moments later Jess was to regret boosting her mother's confidence with thoughtless compliments. A sweaty waiter approached.

"Would you like to see the dessert menu?" he asked. And Jess's mum looked up at him and—horrors!—winked roguishly.

"Some would say we were sweet enough already," she quipped. "But I have to admit I am secretly yearning for a slice of passion fruit pavlova." And the way she said "passion fruit" in a deep husky voice suggested she would quite like it if he brought it up to her in bed. Where she would be waiting in a pink silk negligee.

Thank God Jess secretly knew that her mother possessed no negligees, and always wore a rugby shirt in bed. She hadn't been planning on having a pudding, but the ordeal of having to watch her mum flirt again made her feel weak with shock, and only a portion of sticky toffee pudding could put strength back into her sinews.

"OK, well, let's get an early night, because in the morning we're off to Berry Pomeroy Castle," said Mum, after the coffee. "The most haunted place in England." A thrill ran down Jess's spine. She wondered what spooky experiences would be awaiting her tomorrow. Little did she know that, in the haunted tower, she was going to hear something that would make her hair stand on end with terror.

18

*J*ess woke next morning to the sound of rain. Perfect weather for visiting a haunted castle. The first thing she did, as usual, was to grab her mobile and walk around the hotel until she found a place where her phone worked. A text had come during the night! Two texts, in fact! Darling Fred! A text from him was the perfect start to her day. But wait! Neither of them was from Fred. One was from Dad, and one from Flora.

CLEAVAGES ARE NOT MY STRONG POINT, said Dad's text. WHAT REALLY MATTERS IS A PERSON'S INNER BEAUTY, AND WHETHER THEIR FEET SMELL OF CHEESE. AS FOR THE PUPPY, DON'T HOLD YOUR BREATH. YOU MIGHT HAVE TO SETTLE FOR A CUTE FLUFFY HEARTHRUG.

Jess sighed. Her tragic lack of a puppy was just one more disappointment in what was turning out to be a very deprived existence. Now for Flora's text. Flora, of course, had a fabulous dog called Lucky. Lucky was almost as impossibly blond as Flora, though her nose was a little blacker and wetter than Flora's.

HI BABE! HW'S YR TRIP? said Flora's text. HPE HNKY-DRY. GUESS WOT! I'M GNG TO RIVERDENE AFTA ALL! FREYA'S CMING WITH ME, TO "LK AFTR" ME. WE'RE LVING TOMORO. BRILL OR WHA? I'LL KEEP YA PSTED. LVE, FLO.

Jess felt a terrific pang of jealousy. How she would have enjoyed a trip to Riverdene with Flora and Freya. Still, at least if Flora was at Riverdene she'd be safely out of Fred's way.

STILL GOD'S LITTLE FAVORITE, EH? WELL, ENJOY! she replied. I AM STUCK HERE IN A GRIM HOTEL IN THE RAIN. MY SHOWER CURTAIN SMELLS LIKE AN OLD TRAMP AND MY MUM KEEPS FLIRTING HIDEOUSLY WITH THE WAITERS.

There was a waitress at breakfast, thank God. Lover boy with the gleaming brow must be off duty. Anyway, Mum didn't seem in such a flirtatious mood this morning. She wanted an early start.

As they paid the bill, the gentle rain modulated into a sudden, violent storm. Torrents of muddy water raced down the steep hill, lightning flashed, and thunder echoed round the hills. Jess's mum held an umbrella over Granny as she climbed into the car. Jess leapt into the back and slammed the car door. By the time Jess's mum got round to the driver's seat, her hair was wet through. She looked like a scarecrow.

Jess was glad Fred wasn't here to observe this pitiful sight.

"Goodness! What a storm!" said Granny. "I feel quite chilled!" In the back of the car was a tartan rug. Jess passed it through to Granny in the front. She received it eagerly and wrapped it round her legs.

"I might not get out at the next place if it's raining, Madeleine," she said. "I'll just sit in the car, if that's all right with you."

"Yes, fine," said Jess's mum. "I still want to go and see this place, though. I've—"

"—always wanted to go there!" shouted Jess in Mum's voice. They all laughed. It was the first time Jess had made them laugh for ages.

"By the way, I had a text from Flora this morning," she said. "She's going to Riverdene after all—with her big sister."

"Ah, well, that's a different story altogether," said Mum. "Freya's such a sensible girl."

Huh! What did Mum know? Once Freya had been so mad about a boy, she had gone to a mystic and asked her for a love spell. Plus—and this was such a dark secret even Freya's dad didn't know—she had celebrated her first term at Oxford by having a pig in high heels tattooed on her backside.

"I expect you miss Flora very much, dear," said Granny as they drove through the torrential rain, out of the town and into hilly countryside.

"Yeah, but at least we can keep in touch via texts," said Jess with extreme cunning. So far she had managed to disguise all Fred's texts as Flora's.

They followed the signs to Berry Pomeroy, and almost immediately found themselves driving along a narrow claustrophobic track through a wood. So this was the most haunted place in England. For the first time on the whole trip, Jess was actually looking forward to seeing something her mum wanted to show her.

At the end of the long wooded drive they emerged into a sort of clearing. There was a car park sheltered by dripping trees, and a short distance away the ruins of the castle rose, ghastly, dark, and fractured, into the sky. Jess's mum parked the car, and just as they were getting out, the rain stopped with almost spooky suddenness.

"I'm still not coming round it," said Granny. "I bought this newspaper two days ago and I haven't finished it yet."

"OK," said Mum. "We won't be long."

Mum bought a couple of tickets from a man in a booth, and Jess looked up at the towering ruins. Strange, twisting vapors rose from the ancient stones. The whole place was steaming in a really eerie way.

" '*Berry Pomeroy Castle,*' " said her mum, reading from a guidebook, " '*was built in the late fifteenth century as a main family seat of the Pomeroys.* . . .' Wait a minute, that's a bit boring . . . '*It was abandoned sometime between 1688 and 1701, and was left to fall into decay. It quickly became overgrown and steeped in mystery, folklore, and legends.*' "

"Look, Mum," said Jess. "Do you mind if I just wander about on my own? No offense, right? I just want to sort of tune in to the atmosphere. I can read the guidebook myself. You don't have to read it for me."

"Hah!" said her mum. "You, read a guidebook? All

right. I'll shut up." She smiled. "I'll read it, and if there's anything you want to know, just ask."

"Thanks. See you in a minute," said Jess, and walked off. She looked around. Broken, ruined walls towered above her on all sides. Some rooks cawed in the nearby wood, and their calls echoed round the walls in a sinister way.

Jess walked off to the right, through a ruined doorway, down a gravel path to a round tower with a strange, empty window that looked, somehow, as if it was scowling. Dripping spiral steps led downwards inside the tower. At the bottom was a sandy floor. A draft of air passed across Jess's face. She felt cold and horribly lonely.

Suddenly she felt she wanted to talk to Fred. She hadn't had a text from him for ages. She got out her mobile and rang him on his. There was no reply. It was switched through to voice mail.

Jess didn't leave a message. She didn't want to sound like an idiot—desperate and needy. Instead, she had a brilliant idea. She would ring him at home! He probably hadn't gone out to work yet—most of the catering jobs seemed to be at lunchtime or in the evenings. At this time of day—midmorning—he was bound to be at home.

Her fingers shook with excitement as she dialed Fred's home number. She could hear it ringing in that divine house where Fred's magical presence was a daily reality. Then, suddenly, somebody picked up. It was Fred's mum.

"Anne Parsons?"

"Oh, hello, this is Jess. Is Fred there, please?"

"Oh, hi, Jess! No—I'm afraid he's gone away for a few days."

"Oh—I thought he had a job?"

"No—he got the sack yesterday for spilling things and not being polite enough. Honestly, what an idiot! So he's gone off to Riverdene with somebody—Luke, I think."

Jess's heart leapt in shock. Fred was going to Riverdene! He was bound to meet Flora there. Unless—and at this thought an icy spear seemed to stab right through her heart—unless he and Flora had *hatched a secret plan to go together.*

* 19 *

eroically Jess attempted to continue the conversation in a skittish, lighthearted way, even
though her heart lay shattered into three thousand pieces at her feet. No, four thousand. Eat your heart
out, Thomas Hardy.

"Oh, right. OK! Thanks! It was nothing urgent!" said Jess,
trying to sound carefree and relaxed. So Fred hadn't sold the
Riverdene tickets after all! What a liar. She felt sick, sick, sick.

"Are you having a lovely time?" asked Fred's mum.

"Yes," said Jess, between clenched teeth. "It's brilliant!
Sorry—I have to go now—I'm running out of credit."

She hung up. As she put the mobile back in her pocket,
she heard her mother's footsteps up above. She came carefully down the wet stone stairs. Jess hoped she hadn't overheard the phone call.

"Oh, Jess!" said Mum, as she arrived at the bottom of the tower. "There you are! I thought I'd lost you. What's the matter, love? You look pale."

"It's nothing," said Jess, trying to hide her shaking hands. Fred and Flora, together at Riverdene! "I just . . ." Jess scrambled for an explanation. "I felt a bit odd down here, that's all."

"Let's go up and get a cup of tea in the little café," said Mum. "That'll put you right."

How typical of Mum, Jess thought. *The idea that a cup of brown water is going to bring me back from the edge of madness.*

They sat down outside the tiny café by the entrance, and Jess had a cup of hot chocolate. It might not perform therapeutic miracles, but it was certainly more interesting than tea.

"That tower—the one you were in—is called St. Margaret's Tower," said Mum, consulting the guidebook. "It's one of the oldest parts of the castle. And the basement, it says here, '*is allegedly haunted by the "White Lady," the ghost of Lady Margaret Pomeroy who, according to legend, was imprisoned here by her jealous sister, Lady Eleanor. Several people claim to have seen her or felt her presence in the tower.*' So maybe it was the White Lady who spooked you down there."

"Maybe," said Jess. It was interesting that the tower had been the scene of intense hostility between sisters, though. If Flora stole Fred, Jess would immediately rent a concrete mixer and wall her up alive. Not for her whole life, necessarily. Just until she started to lose her looks. Although knowing Flora's luck, she would still be ravishingly beautiful at ninety.

After the cup of hot chocolate, Jess made a massive effort and assured her mum that she had fully recovered from her haunting.

"I don't believe in ghosts anyway," said Mum firmly as they walked back to the car.

"Mum! You're glued to *Most Haunted* on TV every Tuesday night!" said Jess. "You're a sucker for all that stuff." Jess was thinking how easy it was to be haunted by one's two best friends in broad daylight. She could see them clearly right now, frolicking flirtatiously at Riverdene.

"Goodness, are you back already?" said Granny as they arrived at the car. "I had a lovely talk with a woman who was walking her dog. He was called Bosun and apparently he's fathered thirty-six pups. She showed me her pooper-scooper. It was a very stylish one. She said she'd bought it in New York."

Mum climbed into the car and peered over her glasses at the road map.

"What do you say?" asked Mum. "Where shall we go next? What do you fancy? Garden history, a stately home, or a zoo?"

"I'm getting a bit tired, what with all this rambling about, dear," said Granny. "Sorry to be a nuisance, but I'd quite like to go somewhere and stay put for a bit. All this packing and unpacking is exhausting. I keep sleeping through the six o'clock news."

"I'd like to stay put somewhere too," said Jess. "Somewhere by the sea." She was longing to go and sit staring at the waves for hours and hours. And, possibly, throw herself in.

"Couldn't we go down to Mousehole?" inquired Granny. Mousehole was the sweet little fishing village where she and Grandpa had had their honeymoon.

"I want to go to Mousehole too!" said Jess. Even in the depths of her misery she still retained an affection for small fluffy rodents. Although rats were quite a different matter—especially if they were also one's best friends. "Or even better—St. Ives! I'm dying to see Dad again."

"Well, I suppose we could go straight down to Penzance," said Mum. "That's just next door to Mousehole. I could sort out the accommodation with a couple of phone calls. We could settle down there for the weekend. You two could hang around Penzance and Mousehole as much as you like, and I could drive back up the coast and have a look at the gardens and things by myself. It's not far. I could easily make a day trip of it."

"Great idea, Mum!" said Jess. "You know you always enjoy visiting gardens much more when you're by yourself." Jess liked the idea of whole long solitary days by herself. It would make it much easier to be picturesquely miserable.

"I do wish you'd get interested in gardens, though," sighed her mum.

"Mum, get real! I'm a teenager, for God's sake! If I was interested in gardens at my age I would be some kind of social misfit!"

Mum made the phone calls and sorted out the accommodation—she had a mobile for emergencies. Then they drove off from the haunted castle—Jess had a last look at it, over her shoulder—and within half an hour they came to a dual carriageway down which cars were whooshing with carefree speed.

"Can I have a look at the map, Granny?" asked Jess. Mum didn't need any more navigating now they were on the main road. Granny passed the map back, and Jess picked it up and studied it. Penzance didn't look very far from St. Ives at all.

Maybe, inspired by Granny's example of romance in Cornwall, Mum and Dad would fall in love all over again.

Jess uttered a silent prayer. *God, are you in charge of dating? If so, could you fix it so my mum and dad get together again? And we could all live by the sea in a big house with a huge dog called Boss. And please, please make Flora smell just awful, if you don't mind. Just during Riverdene.*

Although it might be a smart move to inflict dire body odor on Flora for the rest of her fabulous life.

"I've been reading this guidebook," said Granny. "And it's quite amusing. Guess what it says about Mousehole! *'The fishermen of Mousehole once had a reputation for smuggling, bad language, drunkenness and lechery which was envied by quieter men.'* He's very interesting, this writer. What's his name? Darrell Bates. Do you know him, dear?"

"Only in my capacity as a librarian," said Mum. "We've never actually dated, or anything."

"If you could date a writer, any writer, who would it be?" asked Jess.

"Dead or alive?" asked Mum.

"Well, knowing you, Mum, dead would be first choice, obviously—but you could just force yourself for once and go out with somebody who still has a pulse."

"Oh no," said Mum, dismissing the whole of live mankind, "give me Shakespeare, any day."

So all Jess had to do was persuade her dad to shave his head, grow a beard, wear wrinkly tights, and write several works of surpassing genius. It should be a piece of cake.

∗ *20* ∗

fter a while, Jess managed to stop feeling torn apart by jealousy for a split second. She stopped worrying about nightmare scenarios from Riverdene. Instead she was wondering about what Dad's house would be like. Then Mum announced that she was getting a bad headache.

"I'm going to have to stop somewhere here for the night," she said. "I'll have to ring the guesthouse down in Penzance again and say we're arriving tomorrow instead. I hope they won't be cross."

Almost immediately they saw a sign advertising a farmhouse B and B. They turned off the main road and followed signs to a farmhouse. The door was opened by a big woman with a red face, who was surrounded by three fat and drooling Labradors.

"I only got the family room available, dear," said the farmer's wife in a mooing sort of voice.

"That's fine, fine," said Mum, clutching her brow with a tragic air.

"This way, then," said the farmer's wife, and they followed her up a gloomy old staircase onto an ancient landing with low beams. It looked almost as haunted as Berry Pomeroy Castle.

"In here," said the woman, throwing open a low door. The bedroom was long and low-ceilinged with three beds, and it smelt faintly of wet dogs. "The bathroom's across the landing." They were shown a grubby little cubicle in which there was a light brown cracked plastic bath dating back to the 1970s.

"Lovely, thank you so much," said Mum. "Terrific, super."

"I'll leave you to it, then," said the farmer's wife. "Would you like a cup of tea?"

"A bit later, please, that would be marvelous," said Mum. "I'd just like half an hour's sleep first." They went back into their bedroom. Mum sat down on one of the beds and got her headache pills out.

"I'm so sorry," she croaked. "I'll be OK in the morning."

"Don't you fret, dear, I'll get you a wet flannel," said Granny.

Jess went back downstairs to bring the bags up. Deep gloom had descended on her soul. She had been so looking forward to arriving at the seaside and staying there, and seeing her dad very soon. And now they were marooned in this hellhole for the rest of the day.

Jess had a tiny single bed in the corner of Mum's and

Granny's room. It was a bit of a squash. She smuggled her mobile into the dismal bathroom and looked in vain for a message from Fred. But there was nothing.

Mum lay down with a wet flannel on her head, and Granny had a little nap too. The curtains were drawn. It was like a field hospital from a war movie. Jess had to get out. She crept down the stairs and went outside. There was a notice which said WALK WHEREVER YOU LIKE BUT PLEASE CLOSE THE GATES AND BEWARE OF THE BULL!

Outside the farmhouse were fields, and she wandered into the first one, having first made sure there were no mad cows or ferocious sheep poised to strike.

Being in a huge field made her only too aware of the fact that Fred and Flora were together in a huge field too—at Riverdene. Instantly an awful hallucination sprang up in her mind.

"I'd love to live in the tropics," said Flora, looking ravishing with the sun behind her and daisy chains in her hair. "In a house with a big wooden veranda overlooking a coconut grove," Flora went on, stretching her lovely brown arms in the sun. "I'd have a hammock and I'd feed parrots with mangos from my own mango tree."

"I suppose you'd have a swimming pool and a tennis court?" said Fred, clearly imagining Flora playing tennis— or possibly water polo.

"Oh yes! But I suppose," Flora went on, "what with my blond hair and my blue eyes, I must be careful not to get skin damage." Fred was staring at her in fascination, the swine.

"Yes," he mused. "Unlike Jess, who is so very dark, short,

97

and, let's be honest, a bit of a lardass. I've always wondered, Flora, how it is you manage to be so fragrant, whereas Jess, unfortunately—bless her heart—smells rather like a ham that has been left out of the fridge for too long."

Jess banished the horrible idea from her mind. She hated being trapped in these vile thoughts. There was only one way to discover whether Fred and Flora had indeed met at Riverdene, and that was to ring them. She got out her mobile phone again. She dialed Fred. It was switched off. She dialed Flora. Hers was switched off too.

Suddenly a text from her dad came through. MUM SAID YOU'LL BE HERE ON TUESDAY. CAN'T WAIT! WHAT SORT OF JUNK FOOD DO YOU LIKE THESE DAYS? PERSONALLY I'M INTO PEANUTS. I GO ROUND TOWN STEALING FROM ALL THE BIRD TABLES.

Jess grinned, and composed a list: NACHOS WITH CHEESE AND DIPS, COKE, CHEESEBURGERS WITH DOUBLE FRIES, PIZZA WITH SALAMI ON TOP, JACKET POTATO WITH CHILI. WELL, THAT'S WHAT I HAD FOR BREAKFAST, ANYWAY.

She pressed the SEND button but the phone bleeped maliciously and a message flashed up: MESSAGE NOT SENT THIS TIME. Oh no! She'd run out of credit *again*. If only she had a subscription phone instead of pay-as-you-go. And where was the nearest town, where she could top up her account? Miles away. At this point a cloud should have covered the sun, or a squall of rain hit Jess on the brow. But the sun just went on shining in a relentless kind of way. Jess reached a stile that led into the next field. She climbed up and looked over the hedge.

Less than three yards away was an enormous bull. He turned his massive head and looked at her with horrid, mad little pink eyes. Jess turned back, jumped down, and ran like hell back to the house. The farmer's wife was feeding some hens in the yard.

"Your granny is sitting out in the garden, dear, and your mum's asleep," said the farmer's wife. Jess went round the house and found Granny sitting on a little stone terrace, under a sun umbrella, sipping tea.

"Hello, love!" said Granny, beaming. "Mrs. Hawkins brought me these cakes. Have one, dear."

Jess sat down by Granny and accepted a cake. How easy it would be to slide into binge eating as a cure for a broken heart. She stared at the flower beds without even seeing them. Her mind was a hundred miles away, in Riverdene.

"Are you all right, dear?" asked Granny. She was leaning towards Jess, peering into her face like Miss Marple.

"Fine, thanks, Granny!" replied Jess, trying to back it up with a bright smile. But she could feel the smile losing its power and fading like a torch with a flat battery. Granny frowned.

"Something's the matter, dear. Come on! Spit it out! I may not be able to put things right but it always helps to talk."

Jess hesitated. She wouldn't dare to mention Fred to her mum, but what about Granny? She was a lot less fierce on the subject of men and boys. In fact, in her way, she found them kind of cute.

"Granny . . . ," said Jess hesitantly, "did you ever . . . when you and Grandpa were young . . . were you ever jealous of other girls?"

"Was I jealous?" exclaimed Granny. And she threw back her head and laughed. "I'll never forget Christine Elliott. She was a dark girl with a sort of snaky smile. She tried to steal him off me. It was on the annual office trip to the seaside. It was in the days of miniskirts, dear. It must have been about 1964. Goodness! It seems like yesterday."

"What happened?" asked Jess.

"Well, Grandpa and I were sitting on the beach. I call him Grandpa, but of course then he was only about twenty-five or so. That Christine creature, she'd had too many shandies with her fish and chips at lunch. Then we all went down to the beach, and she did a sort of striptease right in front of us. She had her bikini on underneath, luckily, but she threw her tights right into John's face, shouted *Come and get it!* and ran down and jumped in the sea."

"I hope she drowned," said Jess.

"I'm afraid not," said Granny. "She just floundered about for a bit, jumping up and down, pretending her top was coming off, silly girl. Then when she came out again she fell on the sand right next to John and said *Dry me, John, dry me.*"

"What a tart," said Jess. "I hope Grandpa ignored her."

"He threw her towel over her and told her to do herself a favor and shut up," said Granny. "And I'm afraid I did something awful."

"What? What?"

"I picked up her clothes and ran down and threw them into the sea. She didn't bother us anymore after that," said Granny with grim satisfaction. "Always remember, dear, the beach can be a dangerous place. What with everyone taking their clothes off and throwing caution to the winds."

Jess sighed. It was a great story but it wasn't much help.

"So who is it who's bothering you, dear?" asked Granny.

"Well, promise not to tell Mum?"

"I never tell her anything," said Granny with a knowing smile.

"There's a boy I like, and he likes me."

"Frank?" asked Granny. She always got his name wrong.

"Fred, yes."

"I like him. He's got very expressive eyes, dear. A bit like a sea lion." Jess let this pass. Fred's eyes were certainly large and gray.

"And I've found out that he and Flora are both at River-dene."

"Together?" asked Granny sharply.

"Well, no, I don't think they actually went together—unless they were lying," said Jess. "Flora's gone with her sister and Fred's mum said Fred had gone with Luke."

"I was reading about that music festival thing in the paper," said Granny. "How many do they reckon are there? A hundred thousand?"

"I don't know. But they're bound to meet. There's loads of people from school going and they'll all be texting one another."

"Well, even if they do meet," said Granny, "if this boy really likes you, he won't go astray."

"Yes, but Flora is so damned beautiful!" growled Jess.

"Everyone likes a pretty face," said Granny. "But boys can be scared of beautiful girls."

"Granny!" said Jess. "You were supposed to say *You're heaps more beautiful than Flora anyway, dear.*"

"Well, of course, you are," said Granny. "But looks aren't everything. You've got more charisma in your little finger than that Flora creature has in her whole body. And it's charisma that counts, dear," she added, giving her most charismatic wink.

Jess felt immensely cheered by the news that she had charisma and Flora did not. "But Granny," she went on miserably, "what if they do get together, in spite of everything?"

"Then," said Granny, leaning in close and dropping her voice to a whisper, "we'll hatch a fiendish plot to murder her, dear!"

After this Jess felt a bit better. She and Granny invented a game in which one player nominated a harmless household object, and the other had to invent a plan to murder Flora with it. It very pleasantly whiled away the rest of the afternoon. Jess's favorite murder weapon was the cheese grater, but Granny preferred a large wooden spoon. It took much longer to achieve the desired result, but Granny found it richly satisfying.

Next day they drove down to Penzance, at the very tip of England. At last they arrived at the ocean, vast and shimmering. The town, silhouetted on a hill, looked exotic. There were lots of boats moored in the marina, their masts dipping and bobbing.

Dear Fred, Jess began another letter in her head. Later she would transfer it to paper. We have arrived at the seaside at last. I am making urgent plans to jump ship and work my passage to Panama as a cabin boy with slightly gay eyelashes and a repulsive pout. Or maybe I shall reinvent myself as a mermaid.

Although knowing me I shall get it the wrong way round and emerge with a fish's head and bare human bum—the worst of both worlds.

As soon as I can establish contact with you via my mobile I shall walk on the beach, broadcasting the crash of the waves and the scream of the gulls—a kind of low-budget audio version of Pirates of the Caribbean, without Orlando Bloom, without Johnny Depp, without . . . without the Caribbean, sadly. And without . . . well, without the pirates.

Still, there were palm trees in the front garden of the B and B. Mum turned into the gateway and parked, luckily just avoiding contact with a low wall smothered in flowers. "Here we are," she said. They piled out—quite stiffly, in Granny's case, and went inside.

"Hi there!" They were greeted by a big man with a lot of red curly hair. "I'm Bernie Ackroyd! How's the headache? Better, I hope?" He shook hands all round, causing multiple fractures, and then insisted on carrying everybody's bags up to their rooms, all in one trip.

"I think he's an Aussie!" hissed Granny. "He's got the twang!"

Jess hated the way her mum and her granny both commented on people they had just met, in a deafening stage whisper.

"Granny! Button that lip!" she whispered. She didn't want to offend Bernie. They had to stay on the right side of a man whose grip would immobilize a crocodile.

Mum and Granny had a twin-bedded room at the front, painted a startling purple, and Jess had a double room at the back. The walls were the color of blood to which a dash of mud had been added. It seemed Bernie's color sense was fairly primitive.

Jess didn't mind. It was nice to have a whole double room to herself. She would be able to chuck her clothes everywhere. She could write her letters to Fred without attracting any impertinent inquiries. And once she'd bought some more credit, she could lie in bed and text him all night until he screamed for mercy.

She went back to Mum and Granny's room to ask for some money to buy the phone credit. Bernie was still hanging about and chatting to Mum. In fact, he was sitting on the bed, which in Jess's view was a diabolical liberty.

"I used to be a sports teacher," he was saying, "but then I came down here and one thing led to another."

"How long have you been running the B and B?" asked Mum with a nasty girlish smile. She looked like a twelve-year-old with a crush on the football coach.

"Aw, a coupla years," said Bernie.

"Do you run it on your own?" asked Mum—almost as if she was trying to find out if he was *married*. Maybe she fancied him! Gross!

"Ah, I get a couple of girls in to do the beds and serve the breakfasts," said Bernie. "But I do all the cooking! Will you be having dinner in tonight? I was planning a moussaka."

"Perfect!" said Mum. Strangely, as she had never been all that keen on moussaka before.

"Well . . . ," said Bernie. "I'll leave you to get settled in. Dinner's at seven-thirty if that's OK? Here's the keys. There's a front door key in case you want to paint the town red." And he actually winked at Mum, as he went out! Good Lord! As if he fancied her! How perfectly loathsome! Especially as Jess was planning to get her parents together again. She didn't want Bernie to start intervening. He looked as if he could kill Dad with one light blow of his little finger.

"What a nice man," said Mum, dancing with ridiculous happiness to the window. "And what a lovely view!"

My mother is revving up for a major indiscretion, Jess continued her letter to Fred. She is throwing herself at the enormous Australian guy who runs this joint. My poor Dad doesn't stand a chance. I've hatched a plot to bring them together again. But the Aussie is going to get in first with his steaming Greek delicacies and rugby songs. I have a terrible fear that I will wake up to find he has painted my mother red to match the back bedroom.

Within months I shall have to endure a hideous stepbaby with rolls of lard and red dreadlocks. Unless I can somehow force Mum into a premature menopause. Any suggestions? Look it up for me on the Internet and whizz me a quick text with the details, please.

"Mum!" said Jess. "Please can I go and get some phone credit? I need to know if Flora's OK."

Mum gave Jess ten pounds and in minutes she had found her way to the main street.

Penzance is kind of quaint, she told Fred, in her secret letter, *with high old pavements. If I had any cred at all as a Jane Austen heroine I would hurl myself down a flight of crumbling old steps and then hover picturesquely between life and death for several weeks.*

However, I have other plans. I can't tell you how fabulous it is to be surrounded by merchandise after all those poignant grave-yards, haunted ruins, and remote farmhouses.

She dived into a shop and bought some credit, then walked back out onto the pavement and switched on her phone. Immediately she found a message waiting from Fred. Her heart jumped for joy. She hadn't been able to communicate with him since he'd sent that awful text saying IT'S ROSIE YOU REALLY OUGHT TO WORRY ABOUT. . . .

That was *days* ago. To a certain extent Jess just hadn't replied because she was cross. And her phone had run out of credit—*twice*. So what had Fred got to say? His message had been sent more than twenty-four hours ago.

I WAIT AND WAIT AND WAIT AND WAIT AND WAIT AND WAIT TO HEAR FROM YOU. BUT NOTHING. MADAM, I AM SLAIN.

Jess rang him immediately, but his mobile was switched off. So she sent him a text instead. It said SORRY RAN OUT OF CREDIT. AM IN PENZANCE NOW. QUITE NEAR ST. IVES.

HOW'S EVERYTHING? She managed not to add any jealous asides about Rosie or Flora. She kept hold of her phone, waiting for Fred's reply, willing it to ring. Whilst waiting for the longed-for vibration, she strolled down the street looking in all the shops.

There were some fabulous clothes, and then there was a bookshop where she spent half an hour, and then, right at the bottom of the street, she found a small shopping mall with a branch of the Body Shop in it. Re-*sult!* Jess hadn't had a cosmetics fix since Dorchester, and that was days ago. She spent ages in there, trying on all sorts of different perfume.

You could get Melon, Coconut, or Grapefruit, but you couldn't get Essence of Fred. His skin smelt unique, like hot grass. At the thought of it her legs went weak. Oh, why didn't he reply?

Fred's mobile must be switched off. He would answer soon. She mustn't get things out of proportion. Maybe she should text Flora. She sent Flora a brief text. After all, Flora might be able to throw some light on the situation.

But the whole afternoon just went on unrolling in silence. There wasn't any message either from Flora or Fred. Again she tried to ring Fred on his mobile. It was switched off. Flora's was switched off too. This seemed, to Jess's increasingly deranged mind, highly suspicious.

Eventually, she left a message on his voice mail. "Listen, Parsons," she said, her mind whirling, trying not to sound too cross or too needy, "your mum tells me you're at Riverdene after all. I just want you to know that if you are, I'm going to kill you when we next meet, with the cutlery of your choice. Nah, have a great time. And for God's sake text me."

"*N*ow, today the plan was to go to Mousehole," said Mum at breakfast. "To . . ." and her voice dropped to a whisper, "*scatter the ashes.* Do you think you're up to it, Granny?"

Never mind Granny, thought Jess woefully. *Am I up to it?* She had spent a vile night of uneasy jealous dreams about Flora and Fred.

"Of course I'm up to it!" said Granny, and stuck her courageous little chin in the air. Her lip trembled slightly. "Are you up to it, Madeleine?"

"Stiff upper lips all round!" said Jess's mum. It was going to take more than a stiff upper lip to restore Jess's moral fiber. She desperately needed to have her spine encased in concrete.

Bernie approached the table, frisking and flirting in a way

which would have been quite hard to take in a man half his size.

"You've given up on my sausages, girls!" he complained. "And Madeleine, you haven't touched your bacon."

"We're all a little bit tense this morning," confessed Jess's mum. *Don't tell him, don't tell him,* thought Jess intently. *Don't mention anything to do with ashes or urns or dead grandpas, Mother, I beg!*

"The thing is," her mum went on, "we've got rather a sad little duty to carry out today—to throw Grandpa's ashes into the sea at Mousehole." Bernie's face dropped about 30,000 feet at this news, and the family sitting at the next table hurriedly got to their feet and left the room.

"Aw, bad luck, I didn't know, I'm sorry," said Bernie, scratching his head in rather an embarrassed way and backing off slightly. "Well, I hope it goes OK." What more could you say?

Some people had joyful holidays involving sun, sea, sand, and windsurfing, but Jess was beginning to feel that she belonged to a kind of British version of the Addams family: mooching around gloomily with their wretched urn. As they left the dining room and trooped back up to their rooms, it seemed as if a dark miasma of doom followed them upstairs.

Although Grandpa would have hated anything like that. He had been a jolly cuddly fellow with a deep North Country voice and lovely big ears like an elephant. Jess felt a pang of sorrow that she would never again be able to sit on his knee and ransack his jacket pockets for chocolate drops. Although, come to think of it, she was convinced she had grown into such a porky teenager that for her to sit on any old man nowadays would be an act of the direst cruelty, and would probably result in a broken femur.

"Don't wear your black punky stuff today!" warned Mum, sticking her head round Jess's door. "Wear something cheerful. It's a celebration of Grandpa's life, not a sad occasion. I'm going to read a poem about him."

"Oh, for God's sake, Mum! We've already had the funeral and you read a poem out then."

"I've written a much better poem since then," said her mum, looking a bit furtive.

"I don't think it's very easy for Granny when you drag everything out with these poems and things," said Jess. "And whenever you start reading poetry out I always start to feel sick. It's nothing personal. Your poems are brilliant. But I just prefer to read them silently in my head. Otherwise it starts to feel like school assembly."

"It won't take long," said Mum. "It's a very short poem. Now hurry up! We leave in five minutes." And she disappeared. Jess sighed.

Could today get any worse? First there was the endless agony of Flora and Fred holding hands at Riverdene. Then on top of that was a layer of grief: having to say goodbye to Grandpa. Then there was the top layer: her mum, determined to turn it all into some kind of literary festival. The day was shaping up to be a lasagna of horror.

It wasn't more than a few minutes' drive from Penzance to Mousehole. They followed the coast road round a headland.

"This is Newlyn," observed Mum, as they drove past a

quayside where several fishing boats were moored. "Famous for its pilchard fleet and a very distinguished school of painting in the late nineteenth century."

Jess made plans to get her mother an alternative career as a tour guide, and send her off with a busload of Japanese tourists to inflict all this education on them.

"I remember John and I came to Newlyn for tea one day," said Granny. "The café was filthy, it was a disgrace, and the scones were at least three days old."

Jess remembered the sorts of things Grandpa used to say. Something made her reach deep inside herself and produce a comment in his gruff old voice.

"I don't rate these scones, Valerie," she boomed from the backseat. "Mine's like a lump o' blasted rock!"

Granny started to giggle: Mum shot her a very disapproving look in the rearview mirror.

"You've got him off to a T, Jess, love!" said Granny. "Isn't she clever, Madeleine? She should go onstage with a talent like that. It'd be a shame to waste it."

"I am going to be a stand-up comedian, remember, Granny," said Jess.

"Well, I think you'll be a wonderful one, dear," said Granny. "I only hope I live to see it."

"I'm going to drop you two off in the center of Mousehole," said Mum. "Then I'll go off and find somewhere to park, and come and find you."

Mousehole was just a village, with a small harbor almost completely enclosed by two curving seawalls, like arms cuddling the cluster of boats within. Right now the tide was out, though, and the boats sort of leaned over sideways, looking as if they couldn't wait for the sea to come flooding back in and lift them up so they could bob and dance about again.

Jess and Granny got out right by the harbor, and Mum drove off. There was a little bench at the harbor's edge and Jess and Granny sat on it.

"Dammit," said Granny. "I forgot the blasted urn."

"Mum'll bring it," said Jess.

There was a pause, during which a few seagulls flew over them, trying to see if they had any food which could be stolen with a quick swoop and wicked peck.

Suddenly Jess became aware that tears were running down Granny's face. She was crying silently. This was terrible. Although it would have been even worse, of course, if she had thrown her head back and howled like a lovesick Rottweiler.

Jess put her arm round Granny. She couldn't think of anything to say. She just wished Mum would come soon. There should be a law against grown-ups crying, especially in public. And Granny was usually so wacky and playful, it was particularly horrible to see her lip trembling and horrid little glittery bits in the bottom of her eyes.

"Sorry, love," murmured Granny. "I believe this is what you young people call Losing It."

23
* *

"I've been thinking about Thomas Hardy, dear," confessed Granny, rootling in the sleeve of her cardigan for her hankie. "You know, how he asked for his heart to be removed. I wish I'd had Grandpa's taken out. So I could keep a little bit of him once the ashes had gone."

Jess imagined what it would be like if all she had left of Fred was a few ashes in an urn. The thought was so horrid that she burst into tears too, and a ghastly bubble billowed out of her nose. Jess didn't have a hankie so she wiped her nose on her sleeve. It was clear that her feelings for Fred were as strong as ever, even if he had run off with Flora, the faithless swine.

"Don't be upset, dear," sniveled Granny. "I've set you off, I'm sorry!"

This was awful. Instead of cheering Granny up and offering her support, Jess felt she was making things much worse. Instinctively, she reached inside herself again for Grandpa's gruff, deep voice.

"For crying out loud, Valerie, stop that damned caterwauling!" she boomed. Granny laughed through her tears. "Get a grip, woman! Don't even think about meddling with my vital organs. Wanting to carry me heart around with you, the very idea! Knowing you, you'd leave it on a park bench and it'd be gobbled up by a passing dog!"

Granny started uncontrollably, hysterically laughing. Jess was afraid she might have gone a bit too far, but Granny begged for more. "Do it again, Jess, do it again!"

"I'm not saying any more to you, Valerie, until you've stopped that blooming sniveling and powdered your blinking nose," boomed Jess in Grandpa's voice. Hastily Granny got her powder compact out and repaired the damage. She had stopped crying now.

"So where exactly do you want your ashes put, John?" Granny asked, for all the world as if he was sitting right next to her.

"I want to be chucked on the football pitch of Manchester United, of course, woman," said Grandpa—via Jess.

Granny stared at Jess in consternation. "I never thought of that!" she whispered, in panic.

"Don't worry, Granny," said Jess. "I only made that up because he was such a football fan. You wanted to throw the ashes into the sea, and if that's what you want, go for it."

Granny looked out across the harbor wall, and shook her head slowly. "I'm beginning to think this isn't such a good idea," she said. "I mean, look, love: the tide's out. We can't get anywhere near it. And if we came back when the tide was in, and tried to do it then, what if there was somebody watching? It wouldn't be private enough. And what if there was a sudden puff of wind? I wouldn't want Grandpa to be plastered all over the harbor."

"Well, that's fine, Granny," said Jess. "You must do what you want. If you need more time to think about it, take more time. And you don't have to part with the ashes at all if you don't want to."

"Oh, don't I?" said Granny, and relief broke out all over her face.

"Course you don't, you daft lass," boomed Jess in Grandpa's voice.

"Well, perhaps I won't part with him at all, then, ever," said Granny in a determined voice. She sounded much less wobbly now. Jess gave a great sigh of relief. She felt shattered. It was exhausting, bringing people back from the verge of despair. However did professional counselors do it? And when was somebody going to do the same for her?

Mum arrived, carrying the urn and looking rather frazzled. "I had to park almost in the next village," she moaned. "And even then I got some dirty looks."

"Never mind, dear," said Granny serenely.

"Shall we get on with it, then?" asked Mum. "This urn's heavy. Where's the sea gone?"

"The tide's out," said Granny. "And I've decided not to throw Grandpa's ashes in the sea today."

"What?" said Jess's mum. "But I've got my poem ready and everything. This is the moment we've been preparing for."

"No it isn't, dear," said Granny firmly. "Now let's find a café. I'm gasping for a cup of tea and I could murder a cake or two."

After the tea break, they walked around Mousehole. Jess and her mum took turns carrying the urn. It was a bit odd, taking your dead grandfather for walkies. But on the other hand, it would have tickled Grandpa to bits. Jess could almost hear his voice in her head, saying *For goodness' sake, Jessica, let's be getting back. The football starts at half past two!*

The tiny little backstreets of Mousehole were like a maze. The houses seemed ancient, and right in the middle was somebody's garden behind a high wall, with some banana plants poking their great big tropical leaves up towards the sky.

"Banana plants! How exotic!" said Jess's mum. "Like Tangier or somewhere, I imagine."

Jess didn't ask where Tangier was. She'd had quite enough education already for one morning. It was odd how her mum could cheer up at the sight of a plant or two. Jess was glad her mum was looking happier. Because she was planning to cry on Mum's shoulder at the first opportunity. And it wouldn't be fair to cry on somebody's shoulder if they were already depressed.

Obviously, she wouldn't mention Fred. But she was fairly confident that Mum would give her a cuddle and a bit of comfort. Jess would just say she was feeling sad. She wouldn't have to go into details. What with the Grandpa's ashes fiasco, there was plenty to be upset about without mentioning lurve.

They stayed for lunch in Mousehole—delicious fish and chips—and got back to Penzance in the middle of the afternoon. Granny went off for a little siesta, and Mum said she was going to have a look at a nearby park.

"Do you want to come, Jess?" she asked, expecting Jess to say no. Jess was too old for swings, and too young for plants.

"Yes, I think I will, actually, Mum!" said Jess. Her mum looked startled, but accepted Jess's company, and they strolled arm in arm to the park, which was only a couple of minutes away from the B and B.

Flowering shrubs and palms grew everywhere, and Jess could feel her mum relaxing at the sight of so much botany. They sat down on a bench in the shade. *Now's my chance,* thought Jess. She was just about to tell her mum how low she was feeling, and place her head tragically on her mum's shoulder, when Mum got in first.

"I've been thinking about what you said," she murmured, holding on more and more tightly to Jess's hand, until it seemed that the blood would never again be able to reach Jess's fingers. "It hasn't been fair at all of me not to tell you what went wrong between me and Dad. I suppose I've always felt a bit embarrassed about it."

"There's no need to tell me now, Mum," said Jess hastily. She wasn't sure if she could bear any more tragic stuff today.

"No, it's all right, you've been pestering me to tell you about it for ages," said Mum. "The fact is, we were only married for a couple of years. He just—well, he made it clear he didn't really want to be married to me. He just went sort of cold and distant, and a few months after you were born, he moved out. I assume . . ."

Her mum hesitated for a moment, and to Jess's horror, she realized her mum was fighting off tears. Oh no! Not again!

*J*ess's mum got out her hankie, blew her nose, and resumed her tragic account of her marriage breakup. ". . . I think Dad moved out, basically because, well, because he didn't find me attractive anymore."

Jess cringed. She had been pestering her mum for years to tell her all about the breakup, but now the moment had come, it was the last thing Jess wanted to hear. It was way too soon after all that emotional stuff with Grandma. Jess decided to head off this heavy scene before her mum got any more tearful.

She had to be bold. She had to be hugely brave, but if she did it with enough panache, it just might work.

"Well, is it surprising?" she said. "What man could endure your enormous nose like an elephant's trunk, Mum?" (In reality Jess's mum's nose was tiny and cute.) "And your green teeth, dripping with slime, home to numberless small mollusks?" (Jess's mum flossed three times a day.)

Mum listened. For a moment she looked a bit cross that her tragic moment had been railroaded into comedy, but then the corners of her mouth began to twitch towards a smile. Jess redoubled her efforts.

"Most men like their wives to have hair, Mum, not a bald pate like yours covered with tattoos." Mum smiled, fighting off a laugh. Jess was determined to get her going. But it was much harder work than earlier, with Granny.

"I'm sure Dad would have been happy with a quiet woman who liked to spend her evenings reading and gardening." (Jess's mum's very favorite things.) "But frankly, the way you go out and get drunk every night, swearing horribly, beating up policemen and forcing chips through people's letter boxes, would put a strain on any marriage."

Jess's mum laughed. Out loud! *Jackpot!* thought Jess in triumph. She spent the rest of the afternoon assuring her mum that she was the most attractive of all the forty-something women in Cornwall. If Lawrence of Arabia had met her, he would certainly have abandoned the habits of a lifetime and urged her to become his wife. If Thomas Hardy had known her, he would have offered her his heart, possibly even with salad and fries. If Shakespeare had seen her, he wouldn't have written *Hamlet, Prince of Denmark*. It would have been *Madeleine, Princess of Penzance*.

Eventually, Mum abandoned her deep self-hatred and agreed to have an ice cream whilst admiring some calla lilies.

"Thank you, darling, for cheering me up," she said, licking her Exotic Solero. "You are the very best daughter anybody could have."

Jess was relieved, though exhausted. After supper that night, she went straight to bed feeling shattered.

I'll just lie awake and torture myself with thoughts of Fred and Flora for a few hours, she thought. *I've been so busy with other people's misery I haven't had any time to wallow in my own.*

Maybe she should give up all hope of happiness on earth. Maybe she should give away all her possessions and become a Buddhist.

Then, out of the blue, her mobile buzzed on the bedside table. Jess grabbed it. There was a text from Fred! BLOODY HELL! LOST MOBILE FOR WHOLE DAY! FOUND IT IN SOCK! WILL YOU EVER FORGIVE?

Instantly Jess whizzed off a reply. HAD ASSUMED YOU WERE TOO BUSY FLIRTING WITH FLORA AND HAD FORGOTTEN ME. Within seconds she had her answer. WHAT?? FLORA??? WHERE IS THE DITZY NITWIT? HAVEN'T SEEN HER FOR WEEKS.

REALLY? replied Jess. SHE'S AT RIVERDENE TOO—HAD ASSUMED SHE WAS WITH YOU. There was a brief appalling pause. Then his answer came. JUST TRUST ME—I HAVEN'T SEEN HER AT ALL AND I'VE NEVER STOPPED THINKING ABOUT YOU FOR A SINGLE MINUTE. EVEN WHEN EATING.

DITTO, replied Jess. WHO'S DITTO? said Fred. SOME LEERING BEACH BUM? I AM CONSUMED WITH JEALOUSY, MADAM. DO NOT EVEN LOOK AT ANOTHER MALE ANIMAL NOT EVEN A CANARY OR WOE IS ME.

At this point, for some reason, Fred's phone went out of range. However, Jess did feel reassured. Suddenly her phone buzzed and there was another text—from Dad. MUM SAYS YOU'RE COMING TO SEE ME THE DAY AFTER TOMOR-ROW. CAN'T WAIT! HAVE GOT SOME NACHOS IN BUT CAN'T MANAGE THE PUPPY THIS TIME. CAN OFFER YOU A TIME-SHARE IN MY PET SEAGULL. WILL THAT DO?

I CAN'T WAIT EITHER, replied Jess. BUT SEAGULL A LITTLE UNIMAGINATIVE. HOW ABOUT PARROT? NOT SO MUCH A PET, MORE AN ON-SHOULDER FASHION ACCESSORY.

Jess now felt relaxed enough to go to sleep instead of lying awake for hours torturing herself with horrible fantasies about Fred and Flora honeymooning on a desert island. It wasn't what you'd call the happiest ending to the most delightful of days, but it was a step in the right direction.

"I want to have a bit of time to myself today," announced Granny at breakfast next morning. "I've got some thinking to do." She didn't look anxious or tragic or anything, so Jess's mum accepted it without a fuss.

"I got a text from Dad last night," said Jess. "Saying we're going to see him tomorrow. Is that right?"

"Yes, I told him to expect us tomorrow," said Mum. "I'm planning to go to the Eden Project today. Do you fancy coming, Jess? It's a wonderful project with huge biodomes with tropical plants and so on." Mum's eyes began to shine with insane radiance at the thought.

"No thanks!" said Jess in horror. "I'll just hang out in Penzance. I could spend a whole day here just window-shopping. And I might even go to the museum," she added hastily, to make her day sound a bit more educational. Mum didn't give her a hard time, though. She seemed too keen to make a quick getaway, herself.

Jess started by spending two hours in clothes shops, shoe shops, and music shops. Then she wandered further up the main street and found a shop selling about five hundred different scented candles. Jess sniffed 267 of them and then her nose began to feel tired, so she went back outside and strolled a bit further along the road.

There was a bus at a bus stop. People were getting on. Then suddenly she noticed that the destination said St. Ives. That was Dad's town! Jess's heart leapt with excitement. She knew Mum had promised to visit Dad tomorrow, but suddenly she had a terrific, mad irresistible urge. She would jump on the bus right now and go to St. Ives and surprise him!

25

She jumped on, and the fare wasn't very much, so it couldn't be far. They traveled out of Penzance, over open countryside, and finally down a rather exciting road with lots of signs indicating that the magical St. Ives was just around the corner. Jess saw the sea glinting in a great curve of light, out on her right, and then the bus plunged down a steep street, and finally stopped. Everyone got off, so Jess thought she had better follow.

"Is this St. Ives?" she asked the driver, feeling like a bit of a fool.

"Sure is, my dear!" he replied, with a curious mixture of country and western and Cornish pirate in his voice.

Jess jumped off and looked around. She had no idea where Dad's house was. People were queuing to get on the bus. She selected a middle-aged woman with glasses. Her mum had always insisted, "If you have to speak to a stranger for some reason, make sure it's a woman."

In fact Jess had always made it a rule to ask directions from someone who looked as much like her mum as possible. Which was stupid really, as Mum's sense of direction was appalling.

OK, this woman in the queue might be a secret mass murderer. She might try to lure Jess back to her house and make pies out of her. But Jess was ready to grab her glasses and stamp on them if there were any signs of an approaching kidnapping. Anyway, Jess was pretty sure you couldn't kidnap anybody by *bus*.

"Excuse me," she said. "Could you tell me where the Old Pilchard Loft is?"

The woman frowned, and shook her head. "I dunno, dear," she said. "Over by Downalong, I reckon."

"Where's Downalong?" asked Jess.

"Over the other side of the harbor," said the woman.

"Where—er, sorry, but where's the harbor?" asked Jess.

"Just go down there to the end of the road, turn left, and then right, keep going, go down on the left-hand side of the church, and you'll come out by the lifeboat station," said the woman. "Then you just walk around the quayside and round the other side, that's Downalong."

"Thanks!" said Jess. The woman gave her a curious look, as if, for a split second, she was wondering what her buttocks would taste like roasted with rosemary and garlic mash, but then she obviously decided she was too tired for a kidnapping today, and got on the bus.

Jess ran down the road to the corner, followed the

instructions and within seconds was standing by the lifeboat station. The lifeboat was out of its shed and stood on the quayside, gleaming and bright orange. Various lifeboatmen were clambering around on it doing seafaring things with ropes and other bits of kit.

The harbor stretched away in a curve, with higgledy-piggledy old buildings lining the quayside: mostly shops and pubs, all glittering in the sunlight. The tide was out: there were lots of little boats lying on the sand of the harbor. Children and dogs were running around the quayside. Old people were sitting basking in the sun, their eyes closed. Young people were eating pasties.

A Cornish pasty! Jess's stomach rumbled. She went into a pasty shop. She didn't want to arrive ravenously hungry at Dad's house. It wouldn't be very polite to turn up out of the blue, a day early, and demand food immediately.

Jess's mum had given her ten pounds that morning, so she had enough money for a pasty, and selected a cheese and onion one. She bought a Coke to go with it, and went out and sat on the harbor wall. Seagulls screamed overhead, and several dive-bombed her, looking jealously at her pasty with their greedy little light-colored eyes.

Jess had seen a notice imploring people not to feed the gulls, so she sort of hid her pasty inside her jacket and told them to *peck off*. She sat in the sun enjoying her solitary picnic. Music drifted from an open window. People laughed nearby. It seemed a happy place.

She finished her snack and decided it was time to find Dad's house.

"Excuse me," said Jess, selecting at random an old couple

sitting on a bench. "Do you know where the Old Pilchard Loft is?" The aged pair squinted at her, their faces looking like ancient maps.

"Sorry, love," said the woman. "We're only on holiday."

"Is it a restaurant?" asked the man.

"No," said Jess. "It's where my dad lives. It's his house." The old people looked a bit mystified. They clearly thought it a bit odd that Jess didn't know where her own father lived.

"Mum and Dad are divorced," said Jess, embarrassed. "I'm paying him a surprise visit and this is the first time I've been down here." This was getting a bit silly. She had only wanted to ask for directions but she had ended up telling them half her life story.

"Ah," said the old woman. "Never mind, dear. We're divorced too." Now it was Jess's turn to look puzzled.

"You're divorced?" They didn't look very divorced, sitting on a bench in the sun and sort of cuddling up close like a couple of old cats sunbathing.

"We're divorced from other people," the woman went on. "Jim's divorced from Joan and I'm divorced from Harry." This conversation, though more and more bizarre, was somehow reassuring.

"Lots of people are divorced nowadays," said Jess. "In fact, when I grow up I'm just going to get divorced straightaway without bothering to get married first." She had thought this was quite a good joke, but the old couple just looked confused. This stand-up comedy business was harder than she had thought.

"Why not try the tourist office?" suggested the man. "They usually know where everything is."

"Good idea!" said Jess. "Where's the tourist office?"

Eventually, after a lot of confusion, Jess found the tourist office and a kind woman helped her by giving her a street map and coloring Dad's street in green. It was a cobbled street, very narrow and old, with glimpses of dazzling sea between the houses. All the doorsteps were spilling over with flowers and here and there a palm tree flicked its glittering fronds in the breeze.

THE OLD PILCHARD LOFT—suddenly she saw the handpainted sign. Her heart started to beat very fast. She hadn't seen her dad for months—not since Easter when he'd come up to see her in town. The house looked a bit like a small warehouse or a barn. Beside the front door was a ship's bell. You had to pull a rope to make it ring. Jess hesitated, embarrassed about the noise it would make.

There was also a vast brass knocker shaped like a pineapple. Jess didn't want to use this either. It would so obviously be deafening. She knocked on the front door with her knuckles instead. She waited. No reply. She knocked again, so hard it hurt. No reply. What if he was out? Jess's heart began to sink. It was all going horribly wrong.

OK, it was time to ring the bell. Maybe he hadn't heard her knocking. Jess reached up, and tugged the rope. A deafening peal rang out, up and down the street. Jess cringed and blushed. But there was the sound of movement somewhere, far away in the house, and a few moments later, above her head, a window opened and her dad's head looked out.

"*J*ess!" he said, astonished. He blushed. He was so socially inept, the moron. But he was the best dad in the world, so Jess was prepared to forgive everything. "I—I wasn't expecting you till tomorrow!" he stammered. "Wait a minute, I'll be down in a sec."

He disappeared, and the window closed. Jess waited by the front door. She looked up and down the street to see if anyone had witnessed their touching reunion. But, thank God, there was nobody about. So this was her dad's house. It was semidivine. She was longing to see the inside of it.

A few minutes later, the front door opened and Dad appeared, his funny straw-colored hair all over the place. Jess's heart overflowed with love.

"Dad!" she said, and buried herself in his arms. "Big big hug!" she muttered into his sweater. It was what she always used to ask for when she was a little girl. Dad felt warm and safe. As moments go, it was one of the very best.

"So," said Dad, once the hug was over. "You look fabulous—almost human. Where's mum?" And he looked up and down the street as if he expected her to be lurking in someone's garden, crouching behind a wall.

"Oh, Mum doesn't know I've come," said Jess. "I got the bus over from Penzance. We're staying in Penzance. She said we were coming to see you tomorrow, but I couldn't wait!" She beamed up at her dad, and he gave her a nervous smile.

"Well—er—that's great," he said, with just a tiny dash of anxiety. "But we'd better ring her, just to let her know you're safe."

"Let's go in then!" said Jess, peeping past her dad into the interior. She could see a vase of flowers on the hall table. "I'm dying to see your house!"

Suddenly, astonishingly, Dad went pale and pulled the door shut behind him. For a split second he looked completely panicked.

"No—tell you what," he said, "I was just going out—to do some shopping. And I was going to have fish and chips for my lunch. There's a great little chippy just down the road—come on!"

"But Dad—can't I just have a quick look round your house, first? I've just had a massive pasty anyway!" said Jess.

"When we get back," said Dad, putting his arm round her shoulders and setting off firmly down the road. "You may not be hungry, but I am! And before anything else, we've got to ring your mum."

As they went off down the road, Dad got his mobile out and dialed Mum's number.

"Mad?" he said. He still called her that. Short for Madeleine, but also quite appropriate. "Hi, guess what. Our impulsive daughter has turned up on my doorstep. . . . No . . . No, she hasn't. . . . It's fine, really. No problem at all. . . . OK then. Right . . . Well, I might, if the right moment presents itself. . . . Bye then. Lots of love."

"What was all that about the right moment presenting itself?" asked Jess.

"It's a secret," said Dad. "You'll just have to wait and see."

"Was Mum OK about me coming here?" asked Jess.

"Well"—Dad grinned—"she was a bit shirty at first, but she soon calmed down. Probably because she was surrounded by amazing plants."

"Mum should chuck the library job and go to work in a garden center," said Jess.

They cut down a side lane to the harbor and bought some chips and then, at last, her dad began to relax.

Jess was on guard, though. Something a bit odd had happened back there at his front door. It was as if, back at his house, there was something—or somebody—he was ashamed of. Was it anything to do with this *secret* business?

"Let's go to Porthmeor," said Dad, placing his chips inside his sweater to keep them warm. "You'll love it there—it's the surfing beach."

"Dad, you complete dingbat!" said Jess. "Your sweater will stink of chips. Plus you look pregnant, which, let's face it, is unusual in a man." And even as she said it, a horrible idea flashed into her mind. Maybe Dad *was* expecting a baby! With another woman! Or, even worse—maybe he'd *already had one.*

Jess walked on at Dad's side. He was talking about something to do with an art gallery, but Jess wasn't listening. Her mind was racing. Who was back at his house? Jess had seen him from time to time when he'd visited them back home, but she hadn't actually been down to see him in his own place since he'd moved down to St. Ives a couple of years ago.

A horrible vision flashed before Jess's eyes. It was the woman who had taken Mum's place: younger, obviously. No man ever traded in a young wife for a middle-aged one. Incompetent though her dad was, Jess didn't expect him to have acquired a crone.

She was pretty, with blond curly hair and a delightful trim figure, even though she had given birth so recently. And what if she'd had twins! There could be two babies wailing away in the Old Pilchard Loft. Although Jess hadn't heard any wailing when she'd knocked. Maybe her dad's new wife was out. At the family planning clinic, one could only hope.

They rounded the corner of a little lane and suddenly a wide beach appeared before them. Huge waves raced up the beach, and people in wet suits were performing acrobatic acts on their boards before toppling delightfully into the foaming surf.

"I'm going to have my chips here," said Dad, sitting down on the sand. He got out the chips, unwrapped them, and offered Jess one.

"Sorry, Dad," she sighed. "I just can't manage it." She felt a bit queasy, but not because of her previous lunch. She felt sick with dread in case her dad had somehow smuggled a whole new family into his life and not told her.

Obviously, the new family would be favorites. Babies especially seem delightful even when pooing in their pants, dribbling, burping, and yelling all night. How unfair life was. If Jess behaved like that, she'd be in big trouble.

Dad watched the surfers and quietly ate his chips. Suddenly Jess noticed that there was a ring on his finger. She hadn't seen it before. It was silver, and plain, but it was on his wedding finger. Was this the new ring to celebrate his new wife? Was he staring at the waves and saying nothing because he didn't dare to break the news to her?

OK, thought Jess, *as usual I'm going to have to coax my useless parents towards some kind of communication.*

"It's great to see you again, Dad." She grinned.

"Great to see you too, you strange little fish," said her dad. He threw his arm round her and squeezed her tight.

"Some of my friends never get to see their dads," Jess went on. "Eleanor, for example." Eleanor was a complete invention. Jess had taken the name from the Lady Eleanor at Berry Pomeroy Castle. "Her dad went off to live in Los Angeles. He married a really young woman and they've had two babies. Called Carlo and—and—and I've forgotten the other one's name. Bonzo."

"Sounds like a dog," commented Dad, finishing his chips. Oops! Jess must be careful not to make her characters too weird and colorful.

"Yeah, anyway, Elly hardly ever gets to see her dad because he lives such a long way away."

"Curses!" said her dad. "I should have escaped to California. I never thought of that." Jess began to feel that her dad wasn't in the right mood for her serious talk about the postnuclear family, but she plowed on.

"Well, Elly goes there once a year," said Jess. "And she really gets on well with her stepmother. And she adores the babies."

"Look! There's a cormorant!" said Dad, pointing at a large black bird with a long neck, perched on a distant rock. "They hold their wings out to dry them in the sun." Jess sighed. Her dad was mad about birds. Maybe when they got back to his place, she'd find a swan's nest in the sitting room and he'd introduce her to a couple of stepcygnets.

"No birds yet, Dad! Please! You and Mum are always trying to stuff me with education. Let's just go back to your house now. I'm dying to see it. And I need to make a couple of phone calls. My mobile needs recharging. Do you mind? Please may I, Dad?" Of course Jess's mobile hadn't run out of charge. But she wanted to put pressure on Dad to go back to his house. This was no time for watching surfers or birds.

Her dad started to look a bit anxious again. He scratched his head, looked at his watch, rubbed his left cheek, pulled his collar up, brushed the sand off his knees, and then said, "Sure! Just let's watch a couple more waves first." You couldn't miss the change in him. He was definitely hiding something.

*J*ess thought she would have one last try. Surely he'd feel hugely relieved if they could just get the subject out into the open.

"Loads of people in my class have divorced parents," she said.

"Oh, well—glad to find we're fashionable," said her dad, becoming flippant again. But there was a nervous undertone to all this wisecracking.

"There's loads of advantages too," Jess went on. "Especially when the parents marry again. Or just get involved in a new relationship. There's twice the number of Christmas presents, for a start. And two houses to stay in. So kids are really OK about their parents splitting up, as long as they don't fight. And if their mums and dads get involved with other people afterwards, it can make it a lot easier."

Her dad looked keenly at her for a moment. Jess saw reflections of the clouds and the sea in his eyes, but behind all the reflections there was a glimmer of understanding.

"Jess—are you trying to tell me something?"

"Well, sort of," admitted Jess. She waited. Her dad looked thoughtful. Any minute now he would confess all. He would admit he had a beautiful blond bimbo stashed away back at the Old Pilchard Loft, with a possible baby or babies.

"Well, I'm really pleased for her," said her dad. "Who is he?"

Jess's mind reeled, as if suddenly it had fallen into brambles. "What?" she stuttered. "What the hell are you talking about?"

"Aren't you trying to tell me that Mum has got a new man in her life?"

"No, you dingbat! I was trying to find out if you had a new woman in yours!"

Dad looked uncertain for a moment, and then laughed. "Relax, you peculiar little octopus," he said, mussing up her hair. "There is no woman in my life! I'm saving myself up for Madonna."

They walked back to the Old Pilchard Loft hand in hand. Jess was relieved to know there wouldn't be a strange and possibly hostile beauty queen waiting for them, or even worse, a nasty baby who had replaced her in her dad's affections.

"Do you think Mum ever will get a new man in her life?" asked her dad.

This was interesting. It was even encouraging. Maybe this was the beginning of a reconciliation.

"I don't think so," said Jess. "I'm beginning to think Mum hasn't really got over splitting up with you." She peeped up at her dad's face. He looked suddenly awful. Really gutted.

"Oh God!" he said. "Don't say that. I feel so guilty."

"So was it you who wanted to split up, then?" asked Jess.

"Well . . . I think I should leave it to your mum to tell you how it all happened."

"But I want to hear your side of it."

Her Dad gave a thin, anxious smile. "I promise I'll tell you everything from my side of it, but not right now. I've got to have a bit of time to come up with some convincing excuses."

"OK," said Jess, and grinned. "I'm really looking forward to seeing your house. Can I have a shower or a bath, Dad?"

"Sure," said Dad.

They had reached the front door. Dad got his keys out. Jess could see that his hand was shaking slightly. Or did it always shake like that? She wasn't sure. Dad unlocked the door, pushed it open, and politely ushered Jess in. She stepped inside. The first thing she saw was the huge vase of flowers on the hall table.

Suddenly Jess heard a footstep in another room. Oh no! There *was* someone here! She braced herself. Then somebody appeared at the far end of the hall. Thank God! It was only a man. He was short and muscular with curly black hair and blue eyes.

"Oh, Phil!" said Dad. "I thought you said you'd be going out. This is my daughter, Jess. Jess, this is Phil. He's just staying here for a while. He split up with his girlfriend and she threw him out."

Phil strolled across to Jess, grinning, and shook her hand. "Hi, Jess!" he said. "I've heard a lot about you." His hand was warm, and his smile was a mile wide.

"Sorry to hear about—your breakup," said Jess, embarrassed.

"Oh, I don't mind!" said Phil. "It was the best thing that could have happened, really. I found out later she was seeing another guy behind my back. A bodybuilder from Hayle."

"No need to go into details," said Dad nervously. There was a slightly awkward silence for half a minute.

"Anyway," said Phil, "I'm going shopping. I'll see if I can find some little treats." And he gave Jess a special smile. Jess decided she liked him quite a lot.

She had hoped there would be nobody else at Dad's house, but this Phil guy was certainly an improvement on tragic solitude.

"Thanks," said Jess's dad. "Er—come and see my studio, Jess." He led Jess upstairs and into a room with a high ceiling and skylights. Canvases were propped everywhere, and there was a painting on an easel. Last time Jess had seen her dad's paintings, a few years ago, they had been landscapes and seascapes in blue, gray and white, with possibly a bird or a fish.

This time, Jess could hardly believe her eyes. The paintings were a riot of color: fireworks fizzing, bands playing, clowns, sunflowers, jewels. There were still birds, but they were sheer fantasy: pink and purple parrots laying sky blue eggs. There were still fish, but they weren't pale and gray and flat and dead. They were enormous weird creatures of the deep, with flashing lights and antennae and big laughing lipstick mouths.

"Wow!" said Jess. "Wow! Amazing!"

"I've changed my style a lot since you last saw my work," admitted Dad.

"Changed it?" said Jess. "It's a breakthrough, Dad. What happened?"

"Coming to live down here had a big effect on me," said Dad. "Somehow, I felt, well . . . set free."

"You didn't feel free, then, living with me and Mum," said Jess, plunging suddenly into deep, jealous sorrow.

"It wasn't like that, exactly," said Dad. "It was just, you know—as if Mum and I were, well, different species. As if she was a sparrow and I was a—well, a tortoise or something."

"You've got the species all wrong!" said Jess. "You're a heron, and Mum's a hedgehog." It did seem to explain things in a way which was rather cute instead of deeply sad.

"Well," said Dad, "if it's any comfort, I do miss you a lot, and I hope that when you're older you'll come and live with me sometimes. But only when you're rich and famous, of course. I wouldn't be seen dead with a daughter who wasn't in *OK* magazine."

"I'll come and live here with you all of the time, right now, you retard!" laughed Jess. It was only a joke, a fantasy, of course. After all, Fred lived back home, two hundred miles east of here. But maybe, one day . . .

"Anyway . . ." Her dad seemed lost in thought for a moment. "Um—you said you wanted to make a phone call?"

"Oh yes, please!" said Jess. She could ring Fred on her

dad's landline. But could she tell her Dad about Fred? She had better be careful. Sometimes Dad seemed really mad and zany. But she'd never mentioned boyfriends to him and she didn't know how he'd react.

"I want to phone my friend Flora," said Jess. "And Frederika, if you don't mind."

"I don't mind at all," said her dad. "I've heard a lot about Flora, but who's Frederika?"

"Oh, she's just another friend of mine," said Jess. "I've known her since we were at playgroup, but we only got close recently. Flora's really jealous. But who cares? Frederika is ace." Now all she had to do was have a conversation with Fred whilst pretending he was a girl.

Life seemed to have got quite complicated recently.

"Hi, Frederika!" said Jess.

"Hey! Miss Jordan! How are you?"

"I'm just great—I've come to St. Ives to see my dad. My mum went off to the Eden Project today, and my granny wanted a day by herself. I was just walking round Penzance and suddenly I saw this bus which said St. Ives, so naturally, I jumped on."

"God, you're such an action-packed superhero! You make me feel quite limp and drained."

"How's Riverdene?"

"Oh, you know—sixty thousand people all queuing for about three loos."

"I can't hear any music in the background."

"Ah! We're between acts, or something." Fred sounded a bit vague.

"So has Flora managed to track you down yet?"

"I haven't seen the creature. I swear it's true. If I lie to you, may I be changed into a sofa belonging to a fat family addicted to daytime TV and baked beans." Jess laughed. "But listen, Jordan, can you ring me again in half an hour? I'm running out of—"

"Why can't you talk now?" asked Jess suspiciously.

"There . . . some . . . got . . ." Suddenly Fred was breaking up again.

"OK, I'll ring again later!" shouted Jess. Her dad came in from the kitchen carrying a tray with some corn snacks and a dip—and two Cokes with ice.

"Wow!" said Jess. "You drink Coke! So reckless! Mum says it rots your teeth."

"Ah, well, she always was a bit of a health fanatic," said Dad, putting the tray down on the coffee table. "Actually, we both were. It was our shared love of pumpkin seeds and chickpeas that brought us together. We kind of bonded over hummus."

"But now you've regressed to junk food?" asked Jess, helping herself to what she hoped would be the first of many guacamole-crowned crispy things.

"I go through phases," said her dad. "One week I'm on the salad and fruit diet, next week I force-feed myself entire farmyards. How was Frederika? Tell me about her." Jess choked slightly on her guacamole.

"Frederika is great," she said. "She's at Riverdene, and so is Flora, as a matter of fact. I wanted to go myself but Mum wouldn't let me."

"You had to visit your tiresome dad instead. Terrible! I feel guilty as hell."

"Listen, revered ancestor!" said Jess. "I was so desperate to see you that I came a whole day early." He gave a wry smile. "If it had been up to me, I'd have seen you last week, Dad. Last month. Last year."

"You did see me last year," said Dad. "Four times, actually."

"Yes, but not down here in your house," said Jess. She looked around the lofty white spaces, admiring the blue sofa, the blue vases, the light pouring in through portholes in the roof. "It's brilliant! I really will come and live with you one day. And is there any chance I could stay the night, Dad? Oh, please! I don't mind sleeping on the sofa."

"Er, fine by me," said her dad, "as long as your mother doesn't mind. Phil can sleep on the sofa, though. You can have the spare room. I'm not having my divine daughter roughing it."

"Let's ring Mum, then!"

Jess's dad hesitated for a moment, then picked up the phone and dialed Mum's mobile number.

"Hi, Madeleine," he said in a peculiar and rather awkward voice. "This is Tim again. This daughter of ours wants to stay over with me here in St. Ives. Would that be OK? I don't want to mess up your plans."

Jess watched as her dad listened to what her mum had to say—which was quite a lot, as usual. Dad pulled a few faces, winked at Jess, made some polite noises, and eventually rang off.

"It's OK," he said, "although she says she'll get into big trouble with Bernie, whoever he is."

"He's the guy running the B and B. But I'm sure Mum will be able to charm him into submission."

"Great! OK, let's look for a spare room. I think I've got one somewhere, if I could only remember where I left it."

They went upstairs and down a whitewashed corridor at the back, and into a small room with a futon and a white-painted chest of drawers. There was a lovely view over rooftops and a tiny, glittering patch of sea was visible far over to the right, between two houses.

"It's lovely!" cried Jess. "I do want to come and live with you right now after all! I'll do all the shopping and cooking, Dad! No, wait, I've changed my mind, you do all the shopping and cooking. No need to go overboard, is there? I shall be far too busy becoming a professional surfer."

"If you do become a surfer," said Dad, "I'm afraid you'll have to go overboard on a regular basis."

"Oh, I love it here!" said Jess. "Sun, surf, art, fish and chips—what else do you need in life?"

"Speaking of art, let's go back to the studio," said Dad. "I've got an idea for something I want to do." They went back along the corridor and into the studio. "Sit over there!" said Dad, pointing to an old sofa scattered with shawls. Jess obeyed.

"Now, find a comfortable position, because I'm going to paint you and you won't be able to move for at least an hour," said Dad.

"Oh, wow!" said Jess. "You're going to do a portrait of me? That is so utterly cool. Everyone in school will be insane with jealousy."

"Wait and see if I manage to get a likeness," warned Dad. "You might end up looking like a chimpanzee."

"If you manage to get a likeness, I *will* end up looking

like a chimpanzee!" laughed Jess. "I know! I'll try and look like the Mona Lisa! She is divine! Tell me if my mysterious smile sort of topples over into cheesy, though, won't you?" Jess folded her arms and attempted to ooze Renaissance charisma.

As Dad painted, he fell silent. Sometimes they talked, sometimes they didn't. When they were quiet, Jess could hear the distant sounds of the sea, and the screaming of gulls. It was all extremely wonderful—but even in the depths of her happiness, Jess never forgot for a moment that at the first opportunity she was going to ring Fred again.

Sitting still seemed terribly easy at first, but gradually it got more and more uncomfortable. "Oh my God!" said Jess eventually. "I can't hold this pose a minute longer! My back is going to snap in half and my head is going to roll off under that chair."

"OK, relax!" said Dad, and Jess at last let her screaming muscles go, fell over sideways with a hysterical howl of relief, and then yawned and stretched like a cat. Then she sprang up and ran to his easel.

Dad had done a brilliant thing: he had only sketched it in so far, but he had put sea and rocks in the background. It did look rather like the background of the Mona Lisa. And though he hadn't done much detail on Jess's face, he had made her look a bit like the Mona Lisa, at the same time as recognizably being herself.

"That's me!" she cried. "You're brilliant, Dad!"

"Yes," said Dad. "I like the way you look kind of haughty and disapproving. Just like your mother."

145

"But I am like you as well!" said Jess.

"I hope not. Poor child! You've got enough to cope with," said her dad, smiling at himself and shaking his head as he put his brushes away.

"No, I am like you, Dad!" insisted Jess. "In my head!" And she threw her arms round Dad and gave him a big hug. "I shall have to send you away to cuddling school, though," she added. "It isn't considered polite to carry on clearing up while someone is trying to hug you."

"Sorry, old bean," said her dad, and he tossed his paintbrushes to one side and put his arms round her.

nd then suddenly there was a strange buzzing noise. "What the hell was that?" said Dad, looking round anxiously. "It sounded like a hornet." "Only my mobile!" said Jess, pulling it out of her pocket and pressing the SELECT button.

"I thought you said your mobile needed charging," said Dad.

"Bizarre, isn't it?" said Jess. "It's a new one, it keeps surprising me. Now please, Dad—excuse me!"

She ran to the far end of the studio. Her dad smiled, and performed a kind of mime to do with making a cup of tea. Then he went away downstairs.

"Hello!" said Fred. "Behold, it is me, the angel of the Lord, or at least a sort of cut-price low-budget version, which is all that's available nowadays."

"Oh, Frederika!" said Jess. Although her dad was out of earshot, she still kind of liked calling Fred that.

"Why am I Frederika today?" asked Fred.

"Because I told Dad you were one of my very best girl-friends," said Jess carefully. She didn't want to blow her cover in case Dad could hear what she was saying.

"Oh no!" said Fred. "Why?"

"Kittens! How sweet! I'm so jealous!" said Jess, sure that Dad could hear.

"You haven't told him I exist, then? In my admittedly loathsome masculine guise? You haven't told your mum either. Ashamed of me?"

"What, more new shoes! Frederika, you could shop for England! Just make sure you don't step on the kittens. It would ruin your shoes!"

"Enough of this garbage," said Fred. "Listen, for I have a task for you, which you must enact promptly in order to save the Kingdom of Fred from ruin and decay."

"What?"

"Do you remember once you promised to get a birthday present for my mum and somehow you never got around to it?"

"You promised never to mention that again! Anyway, I did have a good excuse—the house was flooded."

"Yeah, yeah, so you said. Never mind. Listen. My mum knows St. Ives, and there's a special kind of brooch she wants from a certain shop, and I was wondering if you'd mind going there and seeing if they've got any."

"Of course!" said Jess. "Where is it?"

"It's kind of hard to explain, but if you just go out into the town I can sort of talk you down. She gave me this old map of St. Ives. I could navigate you like air traffic control."

"OK—just let me tell my dad. I'll ring you right back," said Jess. She went back downstairs. Her dad was sitting at the kitchen table drinking tea.

"I can't tell you how pleased I am that you came a day early," he said. Jess stood behind his chair and put her arms round his neck.

"I'm pleased too," she said. "But listen, I've got to nip out for a few minutes because Frederika wants me to get something for her mum from one of the shops in St. Ives."

"OK," said Dad. "It's time for my geriatric little afternoon nap, anyway. Got enough money?" He pulled out his wallet and gave her a twenty-pound note.

"Oh my God! Thanks, Dad!" cried Jess, startled by this unaccustomed dosh.

"Is that too much?" said Dad. He was so retarded when it came to parenthood.

"Not at all!" said Jess, skipping mischievously towards the door. "It's terrific, it's just what I've always wanted—see you later! Enjoy your sleep!"

"I'll leave the key to the front door under the ceramic toad by the doorstep!" said Dad, as if it was the most normal place in the world to leave a key. This kind of primitive security arrangement would not last two minutes in the city. But somehow it just proved, to Jess, the magic of St. Ives.

Out in the street, she rang Fred back.

"My God, that was an eternity," said Fred. "Now tell me, what's the name of the street where you are?" Jess looked around.

"Hang on a minute," she said, running along Dad's narrow street and turning into a slightly broader lane. "Ah, this one's Back Road West."

"OK, great," said Fred. "Go down it in a northerly direction."

"What's northerly?" asked Jess.

"For God's sake, woman! You come from a nation of great explorers! Is the sun in your eyes?"

"No," said Jess. "It's sort of on my left."

"That's OK, then, isn't it, you pleb?" said Fred. "When you get to Bunker's Hill on your left, go down there."

"OK . . . I'm going down it now," said Jess, venturing down a steep narrow lane with ancient houses on both sides bedecked with hanging baskets. "It's almost illegally picturesque."

"When you come out at the bottom of Bunker's Hill," said Fred, "you should be by the old post office."

She was glad her dad had given her twenty quid. She'd be able to buy Fred's mum a really lovely brooch. Only a few moments later she found herself coming out down by the harbor. There was the post office, on her left.

"Now turn left, then look to the right, and tell me what you see," said Fred. Jess looked. "On the corner."

"It's a sort of gallery, I think," said Jess. "I don't know whether they sell brooches. I think it's mostly paintings and cards and stuff."

"You haven't got to the right place yet," said Fred. "Look beyond it. Go round the corner, to the other side."

"What do you mean, beyond it?" asked Jess. "Beyond it is just the harbor. . . ." Jess went round the corner. And then, she couldn't believe her eyes. "Oh my God! My God!"

There was *Fred*! Right here in St. Ives. Leaning against a railing, grinning all over his face and still holding his mobile phone to his ear. All the waves in the harbor dancing and glinting behind him.

"Fred!" yelled Jess, so loudly that several dogs barked, gulls screamed, and startled babies burst into tears. She hurtled across the ten yards of cobbles that separated them, and threw herself into his arms. "What the hell—! How on earth—!" She grinned up at him. "What in the world are you doing here?"

"Well, I just fancied a little trip to St. Ives," said Fred. "But if it causes you undue dismay, I will of course go home immediately."

"How amazing! How amazing! How amazing!" said Jess, over and over. She simply couldn't believe it. "This is the most fabulous surprise I've ever had in my life."

"I am informed by my astrologer that Neptune is in cahoots with Carbohydrate," said Fred, "so you may find that there are even more amazing surprises just around the corner."

Not even Fred, however, could possibly have guessed how many.

* 30 *

"Let's go somewhere less crowded," said Fred. Jess nodded. At present their reunion was being witnessed by about thirty living beings if you included dogs and seagulls. Fred took her by the hand and led her firmly off towards a quieter part of town.

"Where are we going?" she asked. "And even more intriguingly, how the hell do you *know* where we're going?"

"We used to come here when I was a kid," said Fred. "I'm taking you to the Island."

"I don't know if I have time for a boat trip," said Jess. "I told my dad I'd be right back."

"It's not really an island," said Fred. "Wait and see."

Jess found that the Island was a promontory, a sort of pointy green hill she had seen from the beach when she had watched the surfers with her dad. At the top of it was a tiny chapel surrounded by some low walls, with a sheltered bench up against it. A couple had already bagged this desirable spot, however, and they were snogging away like a snogging machine that had just been fitted with new batteries.

So Fred and Jess just wandered off and selected a random place on the grassy slope, far away from anybody else. It was random, but it was divine. There was a fantastic, panoramic view of the beach, the surfers, and the town.

There was also the most amazing view of Fred's face, and since Jess hadn't had the chance of admiring it for ages, she decided the surfers could wait. Instead she gazed in rapture at his curious gray eyes and strange quirky mouth and ears that were a bit like a bush baby's.

"I'd forgotten what you looked like," she said.

"Sorry if it's an awful shock," said Fred. "You look rather better than I expected. Have you had a face-lift?"

Jess gave him a pummeling, and then somehow they drifted into a kind of trance of staring into each other's eyes, and then a kiss that went on and on for approximately seven days.

"It's the first time we've kissed to the sound of the sea," said Jess afterwards.

"Yes, such a cliché, isn't it?" said Fred. "I'm not sure I like kissing in the open air, though. Not in the daylight. What with all these seagulls and big dogs about. One has the feeling it could end in farce."

"Tell me how you got here!" said Jess.

"Well, I'd always planned to come down and surprise you," said Fred. "I sold the Riverdene tickets to Luke, which gave me a nice little Cornwall travel fund, and I made a bit extra from my distinguished career in the catering business—until I was sacked on day two."

"Amazing!" said Jess. "I never suspected anything. Although I was jealous as hell. Tell me about those low-calorie Sugababes!" she went on, pinning him to the turf. "Which, if any, did you fancy?"

"I didn't fancy any of them," said Fred. "As you know, when it comes to girls I have a savory tooth."

Jess demanded another kiss at this point. Fred went along with it, although he pulled his hood up halfway through.

"Fred, you're retarded!" said Jess. "You're not supposed to put extra clothes on whilst snogging. If anything, you're supposed to rip them off in an ecstasy of desire."

"Not right now," said Fred, glancing anxiously around. "I have this terror of your dad looming up like some kind of Cornish god of war and knocking me unconscious with one mighty blow of his beefy fist!"

"My dad, beefy fists?" laughed Jess. "He's about as tough and beefy as a grasshopper. Anyway, he's back home right now having a rather tragic little sleep."

"Are you sure your mum's safely miles away?" asked Fred, still looking around furtively. He knew Jess's mum was a force to be reckoned with, and feared the deadly lash of her feminist tongue.

"Yeah, I told you, she's at the Eden Project! Relax, for God's sake, Fred! It's so fabulous having you here. I thought you'd gone to Riverdene with Flora."

"With *Flora*? How weird your imagination is, dear child. I had to tell my parents I was going to Riverdene with Luke because, of course, they'd have disapproved of this mad escapade. And at least it stopped you thinking I might be on my way down here."

"Well, Flora really is at Riverdene, apparently—unless it's just another front and she's going to appear any minute."

"I certainly hope not!" said Fred, looking round furtively. "I've got nothing against the girl. I just hate to share you with anybody else even for a split second."

"And I thought you were at Riverdene together!" said Jess, shaking her head. "I was heartbroken, you moron!"

Fred administered a huge and reassuring cuddle. Then they just sat and looked down at the surfers.

"I'm going to learn how to surf!" said Jess. "I think it's a smart career move."

"It looks terrifying to me," said Fred doubtfully. He always pretended to be useless at sports, even though Jess suspected that secretly, he did press-ups and sit-ups at night on his bedroom floor. His tummy was certainly very firm whenever she punched it.

Some little kids who had been screeching irritatingly nearby for the past five minutes ran up and asked the time.

"Six-thirty," said Jess. She was surprised to see how late it was. The sun was still high in the summer sky, and the waves kept on coming and crashing against the rocks that skirted the island. The sea just going on and on like that had made her lose all track of time. And of course, when she was with Fred, two hours could flash past like two minutes.

"Oh Lord!" she said. "I must get back to my dad's. Where are you staying?"

"I've got my sleeping bag," said Fred. "I spent last night

in an old shed-type thing just around the coast path. I thought I'd just sleep on the beach tonight."

"Don't be silly!" said Jess. "You might be mugged or peed on by sea lions, or something. You must come and stay at Dad's."

"There is a backpackers' hostel but it's full," said Fred. "I can't afford a B and B because I used up most of my money on the way down. I tried hitching but I didn't have much luck. My grotesque appearance must have put people off. It took me two days to get here."

"Two *days*?" said Jess, surprised.

"Yes. I slept in a station waiting room on the first night, and in a barn on the next night—which was, of course, rat-infested."

"Oh my God, how horrible!" said Jess, shuddering. "You must come and stay at Dad's. But wait . . . I don't think we should just turn up together, out of the blue."

Getting Fred installed at Dad's was a major challenge. Dad could easily flip, and throw a massive tantrum. However was she going to manage it?

"I can't possibly come and meet your dad," said Fred, cringing. "Men are very protective about their daughters. He might poke my eyes out with a gigantic paintbrush or something."

"What I'll do," said Jess, "is go home and wait till he's woken up—if I storm in there and wake him up, he might be a bit grouchy. I'll just kind of gently break the news that I've got a boyfriend."

"Is that what I am?" said Fred, looking appalled. "Dear me! I had only presumed to think of myself as your minder."

"You couldn't mind a Chihuahua!" laughed Jess. "Anyway, I'll see how he reacts to that, then I'll just tell him the truth—that you've come down on a surprise visit."

"I'll go down to the beach, then," said Fred, getting up

and pulling on his backpack. "Down there. I'll just lie around in the sand hoping to be spotted by a ditzy blonde clothed from head to toe in rubber."

"I hate you!" grinned Jess, giving Fred and his backpack a mighty hug.

"And I assure you the feeling's mutual," said Fred. "It's been well worth coming all the way down here to find you are even more repulsive than I remember."

They ran down the grassy slope and found a cozy place for Fred by some rocks. Jess looked around anxiously. She couldn't actually see any ditzy blondes in rubber, but she was sure they were hiding in a crack in the rock and the minute she abandoned Fred, they would swarm out and ravish him.

"Wish me luck!" she whispered, giving him a ferocious goodbye kiss. Fred reciprocated heartily. Boy, could that guy kiss. Jess felt as if her brain had been sucked out and replaced by fireworks.

"I'll run off now, and I won't look back," she said. "In case this whole thing has been a fantasy."

"I hope to God it has been a fantasy," said Fred. "I don't fancy sleeping on this beach all night."

Jess ran off, back down Back Road West. Eventually it changed into Back Road East. She loved the names of the roads in St. Ives. She loved everything about St. Ives. And she loved it even more now Fred was in it. His blessed presence seemed to spread over the whole town, like the smell of chips only even more delicious.

As she neared Dad's house, however, Jess began to feel horribly nervous. What would her dad's attitude be? She would have to be very, very careful and diplomatic and cautious in her approach to the subject.

As she opened the door—very quietly—and tiptoed in, she almost hoped her dad was still asleep. Though it would mean she had to wait longer to see Fred again, it would also give her more time to cook up a good story. Although wait! It wasn't a question of cooking up a story. Jess was so used to lying—especially recently—that it was a kind of instinctive response.

All she had to do was tell the truth. But somehow this felt much, much more dangerous than lying. It was terrifying. What if Dad went off on one, accused her of being a sly little tramp? He might lock her in her room with bread and water and summon the heavy brigade—i.e. Mum—to take her back home immediately in a prison van with a police escort.

As she closed the door, Jess heard the sound of a radio in the kitchen. Damn! He had woken up. She had to tell the truth right now. She entered the kitchen. Her dad was sitting at the table staring at a mug of tea. A stone-cold mug of tea, untouched. The same tea he'd been holding when she left. This was odd, and unnerving.

"Tea?" he asked, rousing himself and switching off the radio. "In fact, fresh tea. Long overdue."

"No thanks," said Jess. She could not possibly face anything to eat or drink right now. "Did you have a good sleep?"

"No, I didn't even have a lie down, actually . . . ," said her dad. "I had some phone calls to make. . . ." He looked a bit odd. A bit preoccupied. He was glancing round the room as if he had forgotten something. Then suddenly he turned to her and their eyes sort of locked together in a hypnotized stare. Jess's legs began to shake. It was as if Dad *knew*, or something. Had he gone for a walk and seen her and Fred together on the Island? Deep inside, she blushed hotly at the thought.

But this was clearly the moment. She had to find courage from somewhere. She cleared her throat. Should she sit down? Her legs felt about to buckle anyway. Or should she stay standing up? Then she could get a flying start if it proved necessary to run away. In the end she sort of perched sideways on a chair.

"Dad," she said, in a shaky voice. "I'm afraid I have a bit of a bombshell." His eyes widened. His head tilted. He said nothing. He looked seriously scared. "The fact is," Jess went on, "I have a confession to make. I've got a secret boyfriend. He's dying to meet you. And he's waiting, right now, down on the beach."

Dad's face went through about a hundred expressions: alarm, amusement, shock, embarrassment, mystery. It was like a mail-order catalog from the Big Emotion Company. For a long, long minute he said nothing. Then his face settled to a particular look, and to Jess's absolute astonishment, he seemed, well, *sheepish*.

"OK then," he said, at last. "If it's bombshell time, I've got one too. The fact is, I've also got a secret boyfriend. And he's waiting, right now, down on the beach."

* 32 *

*J*ess felt a sort of roaring in her ears. Then her head cleared and the room was totally silent, except for the suddenly loud ticking of a clock. She couldn't believe her ears.

"Do you mean," she said, sounding rather pale and scratchy, because her voice felt somehow shy, "that you're *gay*?" Dad blushed, and pursed his lower lip up in a kind of rueful smile.

"I'm afraid so." He shrugged.

Jess felt goose bumps run all over her skin. How weird! How incredibly weird!

Her brain went whizzing back over the years, remembering times they'd had together. They'd visited the museum, and he'd shown her the dinosaur bones—and all the time he was gay!

He'd taken her to the café and they'd shared pizza and Coke—and all the time he was gay! He'd read her good-night stories, he'd gone for walks in the park, he'd taken her to see movies—and all the time, he'd been gay! In a way, though, although the idea was so very mind-boggling, the more she thought about it, the more she felt it explained everything.

"Well, why on earth didn't you say so years ago?" she said.

She was beginning to feel a crazy kind of relief. She didn't like the thought that he might have actually gone to bed with men and kissed them and stuff. However, if he was straight, she wouldn't have liked the thought that he was going to bed with a woman. One just doesn't want to think of one's parents doing that kind of stuff, at all.

"I didn't—I wasn't—I thought you might be upset." Her dad seemed more uncertain, more tongue-tied and embarrassed than she was.

"Of course I'm not upset!" said Jess. "I'm just—just shocked, that's all."

She started to think of all the cool gay men on TV. Graham Norton. Ian McKellen, who played Gandalf in *Lord of the Rings*. Elton John. Julian Clary.

And her dad was in the same club as these amazingly glamorous guys! "It's brilliant!" she said. "It's so cool! Wait till I tell all my friends! They'll be *so* jealous!"

"Don't you . . . mind, then?" said Dad hesitantly.

"Mind?" said Jess, making a huge, heroic effort to reassure him. "I'm thrilled to bits, you moron! Congratulations! Give me a hug!"

She broke into a dazzling grin, and her dad smiled uncertainly. They both got up awkwardly and fell into each other's arms. There was a cracking noise.

"You've broken my rib, now," said Dad. "This is why I've never messed with women. They have the strength of ten men."

"Of ten tigers, you mean!" said Jess. Then a thought suddenly occurred to her. "Does Mum know?"

"Yes. Well, it became obvious. It was why the marriage broke down, really."

"She should have told me!" said Jess.

"I know—my fault too," said Dad. "We just kept discussing how and when would be the appropriate time, and somehow we hadn't got around to it yet."

"You should have told me years ago," said Jess. "It's a brilliant reason for your marriage not working, don't you see, you retard? I mean, obviously your marriage wouldn't work if your husband was gay. And a gay ex-husband is the ultimate fashion accessory. Think *Absolutely Fabulous*."

"I think I need a cup of coffee," said Dad, moving towards the kettle. "This has all been so sudden."

"It hasn't been nearly sudden enough, if you ask me," said Jess. "Honestly, Dad! You should have told me years and years ago. It would have made perfect sense of everything."

"Well," said Dad, filling the kettle, "I was really mixed up when I married your mum and I thought getting married would sort me out. But it didn't work. All I did was put her through a horrible rejection."

"That wasn't *all* you did, you Muppet!" said Jess. "You

163

created me, your fabulous daughter. Mum couldn't have done it on her own. However, moving hastily on, and avoiding that gruesome topic, I'll have a hot chocolate, please."

Now she'd got used to the idea, Jess was really delighted about it. She was a regular reader of gossip magazines (at Flora's house) and an Internet junkie. "So many cool people are gay, Dad. Honestly. You've got to have a bit of confidence in yourself. What about gay pride?"

"Yes, well," said Dad nervously, "there still is a lot of prejudice about it. My own father wouldn't speak to me for two years after I told him."

"What!" exclaimed Jess. "Grampy?" She was outraged. Nanna and Grampy, Dad's parents, had emigrated to Australia ten years ago, so Jess hadn't seen much of them. They still sent her Christmas presents and birthday presents and talked to her on the phone sometimes, but she wasn't really close to them like she was to Granny.

"It was to do with the way he was brought up," said Dad. "I mean, his parents were born in the Victorian age."

"I so hate the Victorians!" said Jess. "They were so harsh. Still, never mind about them. Tell me about your boyfriend!"

Dad blushed again, the kettle came to the boil, and he made a cup of coffee for himself and a hot chocolate for Jess.

"What's his name?" said Jess.

"Phil."

"What, the same as your lodger?—Wait! I get it! You said he was your lodger to keep me in the dark."

"Well, yes—I had to think on my feet. You turned up unannounced a day early."

"So all that stuff about his ex-girlfriend was garbage as well?"

" 'Fraid so. Sorry, sweetheart."

"What does he do?"

"He owns a boutique. And he's got a little boat. He likes fishing. And he's a surfer."

"A surfer? Wow! And he's down on the beach right now? Let's go!"

"Wait, wait," said Dad. "I haven't finished my coffee. And you haven't told me about your boyfriend."

"Oh, well. There's nothing to tell really. He's just the most brilliant, funny, crazy boy in the world."

"What's his name?"

"Fred."

"Ah! Frederika, I assume."

"Yes. Sorry I lied, Dad."

"Well, we've both lied. It's a shame it's not a commercially valuable operation. You and I could lie for England. We could found a company called Lie-U-Like."

"Or Lies'R'Us! I lied about all those school friends of mine too. You know—Eleanor whose mum went to live in California and had two babies called Carlo and something or other."

"I thought it was her dad who went to California?"

"Possibly, possibly, Dad. Who cares? I was only trying to make it easier for you to tell me you had a new wife and revolting baby."

"Well, you were barking up the wrong tree, there."

"Well, I'm dying to see him again! Let's go now!"

"And I'm going to meet Fred," said Dad, looking apprehensive. "I hope he's not somebody you picked up on the beach?"

"Don't be a moron, Dad," said Jess. "I've known Fred all my life. We met at playgroup when I was about three and a half. He hit me over the head with an inflatable bus and we've been best mates ever since."

"And what's he like?"

"Well, to be honest Dad, I think he's a little bit like you. Sort of useless, and amusing."

"God help the poor lad, then," sighed her dad. He finished his coffee, washed up the mugs, and then turned to Jess with a big smile.

"Come on, then," he said. "Let's get it over with. Although frankly I would rather eat a live porcupine than meet a boyfriend of yours."

"Likewise, I'm sure," said Jess. "I'd rather eat a live bison."

They went out and strolled hand in hand down the higgledy-piggledy whitewashed lanes of St. Ives. When they were nearly at the beach, Jess stopped for a minute.

"Just promise me one thing," she said. "I don't want you to do any of that hand-holding or kissing or anything with Phil. It's not because you're gay or anything. I'd hate it even more if he was a woman. Ugh! Gross!"

"I totally agree," said Dad. "And likewise you and Fred must stay at least three inches apart at all times. Or I might revert into a bad-tempered Victorian tyrant and lock you in a tower and throw Fred to the hounds."

"It's a deal," said Jess. Although it was reassuring to

know that if she and Fred did forget this vow and accidentally brush up against each other, their penalty would at least be gruesome and picturesque.

They arrived at the beach. Fred was sitting on the rocks exactly where Jess had left him, with his hood pulled up. He was looking out to sea.

"Fred!" called Jess. Fred turned and saw them, and staggered clumsily to his feet. He tripped over one of the rocks and sort of shrugged his shoulders about awkwardly before pulling down his hood and revealing his peculiar but mesmerizing face, with its big gray eyes and satirical smile.

"Fred, this is my dad. Dad, this is Fred," said Jess. They shook hands. Fred was almost as tall as Dad, and they smiled gawkily at each other.

"And now, we're going to meet Dad's boyfriend," said Jess. She was afraid Fred might stare, or gawp, or giggle, or something, but he didn't turn a hair.

"Cool," he said, with a totally relaxed smile. Jess was so proud of him.

"So where is Phil?" she asked. Her dad was looking out to the breakwater, where about forty surfers in identical black wet suits were riding on the waves or crashing down into the foam. They were so far away, they looked like little black dots.

"Over there—he's seen us," said Dad, his eyes fixed on the faraway surf. Jess saw one of the black dots coming ashore. He threw his surfboard under his arm, and walked towards them. It seemed to take forever.

* 33 *

*A*s Phil got nearer, Jess thought he looked more handsome than ever. Mind you, emerging from the sea in a wet suit with a surfboard under your arm would bestow a glistening charisma even on a cross-eyed nerd. He was grinning broadly as he came up to them, and held out his hand to her with supreme confidence.

"Jess! We meet again! I'd give you a big hug if I hadn't just come out of the sea!"

"Hello, Phil," said Jess, shaking hands, "Dad's told me all about you two, and I'm thrilled. He should have intro-duced us properly right at the start."

"And this is Fred," said Dad. Phil turned and shook hands with Fred too.

Please let Phil like me, thought Jess. *And please let Dad like*

Fred. And please make Fred like Dad. And please make Phil like Fred. Relationships were such a nightmare.

"Let's go back home and get Timbo to cook us a fabulous meal!" said Phil. Jess wondered for a moment who Timbo was. Then she realized it was her dad. It was a little bit strange to think Phil had a nickname for Dad. But then again—why not? "Your dad's a great cook, isn't he?" said Phil. "Especially fish. The house is even *named* after fish."

"Are pilchards fish, then?" asked Jess.

"A pilchard," said Dad, "is a large sardine. Do you both like fish?"

"I love all fish!" said Jess.

"Proper fish with fins and scales and stuff," said Fred. "But not rubbery things like squid or bits of hosepipe. My favorite fish is the tomato."

"Well, we'll obviously start with tomato salad, then," said Phil. "How about fish pie for the main course, Timbo? With loads of crusty cheese on top?"

"Boring old fish pie on an occasion like this?" said Dad. "The first visit of my daughter and her—er—distinguished companion Fred? It has to be Indonesian stir-fry." Dad grinned, and Jess gave him the thumbs-up, as they walked back up the beach.

"So, Fred," said Dad, "how did you get here?"

"It's one of the sagas of British exploration," said Fred. He and Dad sort of went on ahead, partly because their legs were longer. Jess and Phil followed.

"Are you just going to walk back like that?" asked Jess, amazed as they reached the road and Phil was still barefoot and dripping.

"Oh yes," said Phil. "The soles of my feet are like a rhino's hide. This is nothing. You should see me, running barefoot through the streets in November. It's just kind of macho showing off. So tell me, Jess, how's your trip been?"

"Oh my God!" sighed Jess. "It's been a disaster!"

"Why?" asked Phil. "Tell me all about it. Every detail."

Jess launched into the whole saga. How she had wanted to go to Riverdene first, with Fred, how she'd lied, how she'd got into big trouble, and then the whole trip, with all the jealous torment about whether Fred and Flora were together.

Phil listened closely and kept nodding and gasping and sympathizing as if it was the most interesting thing in the world. "Oh no! You poor thing!"

She told him how Granny had got cold feet about throwing Grandpa's ashes into the sea, and how she'd had to do a ventriloquist act to cheer Granny up. And then how Mum had chosen the very worst moment to cry on Jess's shoulder, when Jess was just longing for a bit of sympathy herself.

"Oh, Jess, you're a saint!" said Phil. "You can cry on my shoulder anytime you like! Not now, obviously, because it's already soaking wet, but in general—be my guest, darling."

"Thanks," said Jess. "I'm all right now, because Fred just turned up this afternoon out of the blue, which basically was the best moment in my life so far. Shortly followed by Dad telling me about you—the second best moment." She decided to tease him a bit. "But what was all that stuff about your girlfriend running away with a bodybuilder?"

"Oh, sorry!" said Phil. "That was just a silly idea. We

170

weren't sure how you'd react. Your mum and dad have been trying to work out the best way of telling you. We've been discussing it for months. We didn't want to upset you." It was weird to get this grown-up perspective on herself for a moment.

"You retards." She grinned. "Still, I do appreciate it."

"And you did arrive all of a sudden, a day early," said Phil. "I suppose we panicked."

"Dad could panic for England," said Jess.

They arrived back at Dad's house and everybody waited whilst Dad rummaged in his pockets for the keys, panicking, for a moment, in case he'd lost them.

"He always loses his keys," confided Phil. "Especially when my feet are freezing." Eventually Dad found them and they all piled in. Phil went off upstairs for a shower, and Fred asked, rather awkwardly, if he could use the loo. There was a loo on the ground floor, and while Fred was away, Dad turned to Jess and whispered, "Fred is funny! I like him very much."

"And I adore Phil!" said Jess. "Thank God! We like each other's boyfriends!" And they shared a quick, ecstatic hug.

"Right," said Dad. "I'm going to cook supper, but you're going to help. Chop these onions."

"Does Phil live here?" asked Jess.

"Yes," said Dad. "We moved down here to St. Ives to be close to his mum. She lives up in Channel View. He keeps an eye on her—he drops in every day, and stays the night if she's poorly. He'll probably stay with her tonight, because she wants her porch light fixed."

Fred reappeared, looking round the house appreciatively.

"Isn't Dad's house lovely!" said Jess. Fred nodded. Jess wondered if she and Fred would have a house together one day. If so, she wanted it to be high and white and blue and cool like Dad's house.

"OK, Fred, chop these tomatoes, please," said Dad. Once cooking, Dad became strangely confident and relaxed. He threw things about, sang to himself, and stirred and fried with panache. His silver ring flashed—the new one that Jess had noticed earlier. She understood now. It was a badge of happiness—without any nasty young wives or rival babies being involved. Perfect!

When it came to cooking, Fred was ham-fisted. His first tomato exploded and covered him with pips, and his second sailed across the room and splatted against the fridge door. Jess found this immensely loveable, but made secret plans to send him away on a cookery course as soon as she'd made her first million. Or maybe they would have a personal chef.

Eventually Phil reappeared in jeans and a checked shirt. He had a 150-megawatt smile. It lit up the room.

"You've seen me in my surfing gear, now you see me in my lumberjack gear," he said, adopting a butch posture. "Now then—glass of freshly squeezed orange juice, anybody?"

"Oh, yes, please!" said Jess. "It might help me get rid of my spots."

"You have no spots! What about you, Fred?" said Phil, pouring out a glass for Jess.

"No thanks," said Fred. "I prefer Coke, actually. I like to stoke myself up with explosive gas at every opportunity."

"Glass of wine, Timbo?" Phil asked Dad.

"Mere wine?" said Dad. "On the occasion of my only daughter's first visit to her old pilchard of a parent? I suggest Buck's Fizz."

"What's Buck's Fizz?" asked Jess.

"Orange juice and champagne!" said Phil, opening the fridge and getting out some of the freshly squeezed juice.

"You can have a glass each," said Dad. "I don't want any teenage drunkenness. Actually I don't want any middle-aged drunkenness either."

Phil mixed the Buck's Fizz with style, pouring orange juice with his right hand and champagne with his left, and not spilling a drop. He deserved a Nobel Prize for cocktails.

"Were you ever a barman, Phil?" she asked.

"I've done a bit of everything, darling," he replied, getting to grips with the Buck's Fizz. "I design things. Cocktails, weddings, fast cars . . . they don't all get made, mind you."

"Phil used to be a designer in London," said Dad. "He used to make fabulous costumes for the carnivals there. In fact, when we met all those years ago, he was dressed as a kangaroo."

"I love Carnival," said Phil. "Sequins, feathers, outrageous wigs, earrings that flash . . ."

"I love dressing up," said Jess eagerly.

"Well, you've come to the right place!" said Phil. "I've got a whole trunk upstairs. Full of stuff. Timbo uses the costumes to inspire his paintings sometimes."

"Oh, can we have a look?" asked Jess. "After supper?" Fred looked a bit dubious. But Phil grinned and winked roguishly at Jess.

"Excellent idea!" he said. "I even managed to get Timbo to dress up on his birthday. We had a fancy-dress party. He came as a turbot."

"I didn't have a proper tail, though," said Dad. "Just sort of silvery, scaly trousers."

"And what about you, Fred?" asked Phil. "Do you like dressing up?"

"Certainly not!" said Fred. "I was born fully clothed in a smart suit made of gray flannel."

"Don't be a wuss!" said Jess. "I'd love to dress you up as a girl." Jess was addicted to comedy shows on TV, especially ones involving drag acts.

"You can keep your pervy ideas to yourself," said Fred, with a grin.

"No, go on, Fred, be a sport!" insisted Jess, laughing. "I think you'd look hilarious—you know, with a long blond wig. Have you got any blond wigs, Phil?"

"I'm not one to boast," said Phil, "but I've probably got the best collection of blond wigs in the county."

"He's also a lifeboatman, you know," said Dad, dishing up the dinner. "He's not all froth and bubble."

"A lifeboatman!" said Jess, in awe. "You mean you risk your life to save people?"

"Oh no, nothing heroic like that," said Phil, as they all sat down at the table. "It was just the oilskins that attracted me."

"He does risk his life on a regular basis," Dad went on. "He won a medal last year."

"Oh, stop it, Timbo!" laughed Phil. "You're not my agent! Get the dinner on the table, missus!"

The supper was divine—a kind of seafood stir-fry, with

174

rice. It was about a thousand times more delicious than anything Jess's mum had ever cooked.

"Anybody for pud?" asked Phil, getting up and clearing the plates. "What would you say to some homemade strawberry ice cream, Fred?"

"I'd say *Pleased to eat you*," said Fred.

"With meringue?" added Phil.

"Fred loves meringue!" said Jess. "You should see him with a lemon meringue pie. He's like a lion with a dying wildebeest."

"We'll make one tomorrow, then, eh, Timbo?" said Phil.

"Sure," said Jess's dad. He smiled quietly to himself. Jess felt this was the happiest evening of her life. She had at last got to the bottom of the mystery of her parents' marriage breakup. Her dad seemed blissfully happy and Jess was sure that once her mum knew that she was OK about it, she'd relax and start enjoying life too. Wouldn't she?

* 34 *

After supper Jess and Fred did the washing up—
badly, in Fred's case. He had been very inade-
quately trained by his mum, even if she did look
like a teddy bear.

"There's still gunge on this plate, Fred!" scolded Jess.
"Wash it again!"

"Domestic drudgery is rather beneath me, I'm afraid,"
said Fred with a maddening smile. Jess whacked him with
the tea towel. Washing up had never been so divine. Maybe
it was something to do with the Buck's Fizz.

Dad and Phil made some coffee and took it up to a sort of
deck, perched among the rooftops.

"You can just see the sun setting on the sea if you dislocate
your neck," said Dad. Seagulls flew around, calling, and some
sparkly little birds strutted their stuff along the balustrade.

"What are they?" asked Jess.

"Starlings! Aren't they beautiful!" said her dad. "Don't say you're getting interested in birds!"

"Certainly not," said Jess. "I was just thinking how nice they would look, stuffed, on a hat." She didn't mean it, though. What she really wanted was a live starling on her shoulder. "Have you got any hats with birds on?" she asked Phil.

"Are you mad?" whispered Phil. "I wouldn't dare—living with an ornithologist." Dad pulled a fierce, bird-protecting frown.

"Can we go and see the Carnival costumes?" asked Jess. "Oh, please!"

"Sure!" said Phil, finishing his coffee and jumping up. Jess followed him indoors.

"You two have got to come as well!" she said, glaring at Dad and Fred as she passed. They groaned in unison, but Jess could see they weren't going to let her down. The Buck's Fizz had helped. Everyone felt festive.

She followed Phil into Dad's studio. He threw a rug off a huge trunk and pulled it out from the wall. Then he opened it. Inside was a treasure trove of fabulous clothes: sequined numbers from the 1930s, silk evening dresses, ancient petticoats, embroidered Chinese dressing gowns, amazing wizards' cloaks.

"The wigs and hats are all in this cupboard," said Phil, walking to the far end of the studio and opening some wardrobe doors.

"Oh, it's fabulous!" said Jess. "Look at this! It's like the dress Marilyn Monroe wears in *Some Like It Hot*."

177

"Try it on, try it on!" said Phil. "There's a screen over there. I'll find a wig for you."

Jess went behind the screen and wriggled into the pink-sequined dress. Fred and Dad came into the room.

"OK, you two!" said Phil. "What's it going to be? Animal, vegetable, mineral? *Lord of the Rings* or *Pirates of the Caribbean*?"

"The trouble is," said Jess from behind the screen, "my boobs aren't nearly big enough for this dress."

"Borrow these falsies, then, darling!" said Phil, and a weird reinforced bra came sailing over the screen. Jess put it on, giggling uncontrollably. Then she emerged from behind her screen and Phil offered her the perfect Marilyn Monroe wig.

"You'll have to pin your hair up first," said Phil, passing her a tin full of hairpins and some hair spray. There were several mirrors in the room. Jess set to work.

"I am definitely *not* going to dress up as a woman," said Fred, but immediately began to try on long blond wigs.

"OK, Timbo, what's it to be?" asked Phil. "A bird? A fish? A scarecrow?"

"I'm in a Gandalf sort of mood," said Dad, grabbing a gray beard. "The great thing about being Gandalf is you never have to show your legs."

"Oh, Fred, you're so Jennifer Aniston in that wig!" said Phil. "I've got a miniskirt somewhere you've just got to try!"

So, in a flurry, they all started to get dressed. Phil fiddled with some CDs and put on *The Rocky Horror Picture Show*.

Jess had found a pair of pink high heels that matched the dress. She teetered about, laughing. She had never had so much fun in her life.

Pretty soon her dad was peering out charismatically from

under Gandalf's pointy, slouching hat. The long robe, the gray beard: he was a role model for the newly retired who wanted to dabble a little in Good vs. Evil.

Fred was looking frighteningly convincing as a leggy blonde, and Phil had slipped into a lime green rubbery suit and a pair of froggy goggles and had taken on the complete personality of Kermit.

"The Time Warp" came on and they all started dancing, led of course by Phil, who seemed to know every move by heart.

Then suddenly, a strange noise broke through above the music: *BANG BANG BANG!* They all stopped, and looked at one another.

"It's the front door," said Dad, looking scared.

"Ignore them!" said Phil. "They'll go away."

They all stood and listened. Phil turned the sound down on the CD. Then it came again: *BANG BANG BANG BANG!*

"Oh God!" said Dad, shivering a bit. "They sound as if they mean business."

"No!" said Phil sternly. "We ignore them. They'll get bored."

They waited. Then the huge front doorbell rang—it tolled away, the sound rolling along all the walls in the house. Deafening.

"I hate that bell," said Dad. "It disturbs the whole street. I'm going to take it down. Tomorrow."

Again the person at the door rang the bell. *DING A LING A LING A LING!* it went, echoing up and down the whole street.

"OK," said Dad. "Look, Jess, you go. You're the only one of us who looks normal."

"Normal!" said Jess. "I mean, look at me! I almost feel like a drag act myself!"

"Go on, love," urged Dad. "Just see who it is, tell them we're out, and ask them to come back tomorrow."

"And keep your wig on!" said Phil. Jess realized she would have to—under the wig, her hair was all pinned and sprayed close to her head.

She kicked off the ludicrous shoes and ran quickly downstairs, barefoot, and opened the door.

There stood her mother, carrying a bag and smiling. As she took in Jess's sequined dress, monstrous bosom, and louche blond wig, her smile faded and her eyes just got wider and wider.

"Jess!" she said, almost speechless for once. "What on earth . . . ?"

"We're just dressing up, Mum," said Jess. A terrible sinking feeling was spreading through every one of her vital organs. "I thought you weren't coming till tomorrow?"

"I just brought your overnight bag," said Mum. "Your pajamas and stuff. Granny wanted an early night, and I fancied a little evening trip."

"Well, come in," said Jess. "Excuse the weird clothing. We're just having a bit of a laugh," she said. "Right?"

Her mum looked puzzled and not as jolly as Jess would have wished. And she didn't even know, yet, about Phil and Fred being there.

"We're just upstairs," said Jess. "In Dad's studio." And she started to climb the wooden stairs. "It's Mum!" she shouted, to give them a few precious seconds to prepare themselves. But she knew, in her heart of hearts, that a few seconds would be nothing like enough.

35

*O*n the way upstairs, Jess felt a tide of rage sweep into her heart. Why did her mum have to come and stick her nose in? Why couldn't she have stayed back in Penzance? She'd always been so discouraging when Jess had wanted to go and see her dad. She'd always postponed it, and made excuses, and put it off.

Now, at the very moment when Jess had finally got together with Dad, and understood what he was all about, and was having the wildest, the most wonderful time, now her mum had to turn up. Hammering on the door like the vice squad or something. Ruining everything.

Jess entered the room a split second before her mum. Dad, Phil, and Fred were still standing there in their fancy dress, paralyzed. They looked ludicrous. The *Rocky Horror* music was still playing, but more softly. Mum looked at them one after the other, in astonishment. Her eyes were enormous. She was speechless. Phil turned the music right off.

"Er—Jess's pajamas," said her mum, holding out the bag rather wanly. "Her toothbrush and clean clothes for tomorrow."

"Madeleine," said Jess's dad, after a creaking silence. He took off his wizard's hat. His voice was kind of high and thin, as if he was being strangled. Fred suddenly took off his wig.

"Fred!" said Jess's mum in amazement. "I didn't recognize you."

"Hello, Mrs. Jordan," said Fred. He tried to produce a smile, but it came out thin-lipped and false, like the smile of an iguana. He looked really rather like an iguana in a miniskirt. Jess was tempted, for an insane moment, to burst into hysterical laughter, but she buried it.

"I didn't know you were in St. Ives," said Mum, and her voice sounded tight and weirdly polite in an old-fashioned way. As if they were all in some kind of 1940s film. Maybe a whodunit.

"I just hitched down," said Fred. "I wanted to surprise Jess."

"Fred turned up a couple of hours ago," said Jess.

"Oh," said her mum, and nodded carefully. Then she turned to Phil, and looked at him in an intense, puzzled way. Jess realized that her mum was trying to work out whether this man in the frog suit was also someone she knew.

"I'm sorry," she said, "I'm not sure if—"

"Madeleine!" said Phil, ripping off his goggles. It was obvious that neither of Jess's parents was, at present, able to organize a conversation. "You find us in the middle of a Carnival moment. A kind of celebration. Of Jess's visit. I'm Phil King." He walked across to Jess's mum and shook hands with her.

"Ah, yes!" said Mum. "I've heard a lot about you." Mum gave him an uncertain smile, and then turned and tried to spread the smile around to include everybody. Dad was still standing uselessly, frozen in his long gray beard, holding his Gandalf hat, just sort of blinking and trembling. It was his house. He was the host. It was his job. He should be putting Mum at her ease. God, how useless her parents were!

Suddenly Jess felt a wave of tenderness for her mum. She stood there looking lost and embarrassed, and also rather shabby. She stood there in the midst of all the sequins and the satin, the ostrich feathers, the glossy wigs—the sort of clothes she herself had never worn in her life. She looked small and sad and real. And tired.

She had blundered into this impromptu party. It wasn't her fault. How was she to know they would be dressing up and dancing? She must be embarrassed as hell. And she had plenty to be furious about. Most of all, the sudden appearance of Fred. It must look as if Jess had been deceiving her mum, and sneaking off without her permission, to meet Fred at her dad's house. As if Dad had been involved in the plot too. Jess groaned inwardly.

But though she had plenty to be angry about, Mum hadn't shouted or complained or even scowled—so far. She hadn't said anything sarcastic, even though her repertoire was extensive. Somehow she was managing to keep smiling, and Jess felt so grateful. She wanted to go over and hug her right now.

But she couldn't, because the whole room had stopped, like a frozen screen. It was as if everyone was bewitched, and waiting for the magic word that would release them from the evil spell. And in a flash, Jess realized that she was the only one who could utter the magic word.

"Phil's Dad's boyfriend," she said. "He's a lifeboatman. And he's won a medal. Isn't it brilliant?"

Jess saw her mother's eyes flicker, as if a speck of dust had caused her a moment's discomfort. Jess prayed that, though Mum must be reeling inwardly, she would say something gracious. She watched her turn, almost in slow motion, towards Phil. She smiled.

"It's lovely to meet you at last!" she said. "I've heard so much about you from Tim. Does he still leave the top off the toothpaste?"

You legend!!!!! thought Jess. Brilliant, brilliant, brilliant! Phil grinned.

"He leaves the top off *everything*," he said.

"What a marvelous house you've got here," said Mum, still addressing Phil. It was her way of accepting that he lived there too. "All this blue and white—it's beautiful."

"Tim completely transformed it," said Phil. Thank God he didn't call him Timbo. It was a bit soon for that sort of thing. "It was a derelict old warehouse when you found it, wasn't it?"

Jess's dad stirred out of his frozen spell. He blinked and

visibly relaxed, like someone moving into sunshine. "Yes, it was an old pilchard shed," he said. "It hadn't been used for years. You could see the sky through the holes in the roof. That's how I got it so cheap."

"And did you do all the work yourselves?" asked Jess's mum, still including Phil. Jess made urgent plans to hug her mother as soon as possible. It was an absolute priority.

"Phil masterminded it," said Dad. "He's a genius with the old DIY."

"Tim did all the decoration," said Phil.

"Although I hate doing the ceilings," said Dad. "I'm scared of heights."

"You're scared of everything!" said Mum, but with a winning smile. "Or is he braver these days?" she asked Phil.

"Nope!" said Phil. "Last week, he was even scared of an ice cream."

"Well," said Dad, "ice creams make my teeth jump sometimes. One doesn't want to scream aloud in a crowded cinema."

They all laughed. The atmosphere in the room softened and warmed. Evening light stole across the blue floorboards.

"Well," said Dad, "I'm feeling a bit of an idiot in my wizard's frock, so I think I'll go and get changed." He picked up his clothes.

"I think I'll get out of this miniskirt," said Fred, hanging his wig back up on one of the wig stands in the wardrobe. "It's drafty. I don't know how girls do it. Next time we do fancy dress I'm going as a tortoise. Is it OK if I change in the bathroom?"

"Sure," said Phil. "Would you like a cup of tea, Madeleine?"

"I'd like nothing more," said Mum. "Thanks!"

"Come down to the kitchen, then," said Phil. "And you, madam." He winked at Jess. "Get those ridiculous bosoms off your chest—you look like a female impersonator!"

Fred and Dad went off to their various changing rooms, Phil escorted Mum downstairs, and the studio was suddenly empty and private. Jess took off her Marilyn wig. Her own dark hair was pinned close to her head. She took the pins out and ran her fingers through her hair, teasing it out into its usual comfortable chaos.

She looked at herself in the mirror. It was a relief, somehow, to see her own funny hair, even though it looked like dark tangles of seaweed. Then Jess peeled off the sequined Marilyn dress, and the bra with foam inserts. Her own body emerged. After the grotesque exaggeration of the falsies, her figure looked almost slim. Not so bad after all.

A wonderful feeling was stealing up from the soles of her feet. Relief. So much had finally begun to feel sorted. She understood why Mum and Dad had parted. She could stop worrying about Dad being lonely. Mum had been nice to Phil. And looking in this mirror of Dad's, Jess thought she didn't look too bad, really. Just ordinary, but so what? Fred had made an epic journey all the way down here to be with her—so she must be doing something right. She grinned at the small, funny, dark girl in the mirror, and went downstairs.

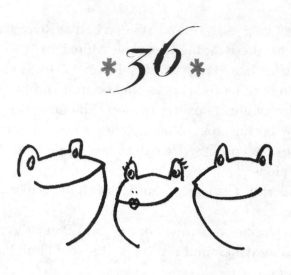

36

*J*ess entered the kitchen. Phil, still in his frog suit, was listening to her mum talking about her day. As Jess came in they looked up.

"Tea? Coffee?" asked Phil. "Cocoa? Herb tea? Coke? Old-fashioned cloudy lemonade? Water?"

"Old-fashioned cloudy lemonade sounds nice, please," said Jess. She sat down next to her mum, but as they were on separate chairs, she still couldn't hug her. If they'd been on a bench, it'd have been easy.

"What are you having, Mum?" asked Jess.

"Apple and ginger tea," said her mum. Jess sniffed it.

"It smells nice," she said. "But I'm not really into herb tea. Flora likes it but I think she's a bit more mature than me in her tastes. She even likes Beethoven."

"Have you heard from Flora recently?" asked Mum.

"Yeah," said Jess. "She's having a ball at Riverdene. You know what they say: Blondes Have More Fun."

"Not true!" said Phil, placing a lovely tall glass of lemonade in front of Jess. Ice cubes clinked in it and there was a slim slice of lime floating on top. "Blondes can be immensely boring, and besides, they show the dirt. We brunettes are far more dramatic." Jess sipped her drink. It was fabulous.

"Wonderful! Thank you!" said Jess. "It looks like a proper cocktail."

"I did work as a barman, once," said Phil. "On a cruise ship. We went all round the Med." It seemed Phil had done everything.

"How interesting!" said Mum. "Where did you go?"

"Oh, Naples, Genoa, Gibraltar, Tunis, Cairo . . ."

"I've always wanted to see those places!" said Mum as Dad and Fred both entered the kitchen. "Maybe I should get a job on a cruise ship—but I'm so useless, I would be the last person in the world to mix cocktails."

"Yeah!" said Jess. "Mum's idea of a cocktail is a cup of tea with half a disintegrating biscuit in the bottom."

"I am the worst person in the world when it comes to catering," admitted Mum. "Do you remember that appalling shepherd's pie I made, Tim?" Dad cringed. "I thought it would be nice to put ketchup in with the potato," said Mum. "But I overdid it. We called it Red Pie at Night— Shepherd's Delight."

"We were ill for days," said Dad, with a grin. There was a brief pause whilst Phil prepared a coffee for Dad and a glass of Coke for Fred.

"How was Granny today, Mum?" asked Jess. She felt a bit guilty at having jumped onto the bus to St. Ives, leaving Granny on her own all day—even though Granny had said she wanted to be by herself.

Mum sighed. "She was a bit low when I got back. It's this business about the ashes. I think she wanted to be on her own with the urn. And I think now it's come to it, she's finding the whole thing a bit harder than she'd expected. She does want to throw them in the sea, but she doesn't want it to be too public. She's afraid she might get a bit emotional, I think. And she's afraid that, if it's windy, they might go everywhere. I think she's also upset because she feels she's being a wimp about it."

"Of course she's not being a wimp! Poor Granny! It's the love of her life in that urn!" said Jess. Suddenly, she caught Fred's eye for a moment. Thank God Fred was still alive and in the same room.

"I tell you what," said Phil. "Do you think she would like to come out in my boat? We could have a little service out in the bay. That would be more private."

Mum's face just lit up with relief and excitement. "You've got a *boat*?" she said. "Oh, that does sound marvelous! Could we really? She'd be thrilled! Thank you so much, Phil!"

Then the grown-ups started to plan the details. They decided they'd do it tomorrow if Granny felt up to it. Jess was sure she would be. It was just terrific that Phil had been able to solve Mum's problem. It was as if there was a kind of magic working away under the surface of things, as if after everything going so disastrously wrong for a while, somewhere a tide had changed and now good luck was flooding in.

Jess had only one thing to worry about now. She was amazed and immensely relieved that her mum had behaved so well this evening. When she'd turned up at the door, Jess had feared she would ruin everything. She'd been terrified that her mum would make a terrible scene. God knows she had enough ammunition—so much to be furious about.

Instead Mum had been quiet and sweet and friendly. It had been really kind of her to bring Jess's stuff. But what if, inside, Mum was still raging? She was a very polite person. Jess could not remember her making a scene in public, ever. She usually kept her outbursts of yelling for when she and Jess were alone. What if she was still seething, under all the smiles?

Jess felt she had two choices: either she must never be alone with her mum again (tempting, but hard to organize) or she must make sure she had some time alone with her as soon as possible, so she could see what her mum was really thinking.

Though this evening seemed somehow enchanted, Jess was terrified that, once they were alone together, her mum would rip off her smile with a horrible tearing Velcro sound. In fact, she might rip off her whole friendly face and underneath there might be a fire-breathing dragon.

This time you've really blown it! She might roar, sparks flying out of her eyes and burning small craters in the pavement. *You're a treacherous, cunning, lying, horrible harlot!* Mum's hair would turn into hissing snakes. Steam would come screaming out her ears and cause a sulfurous fog that would hang over Cornwall for days. Ships would founder on the rocks. Trees would go black and die. Teddy bears' eyes would fall out.

"Well," said Mum, in the real world, "this has been lovely, but I'd better be going." She got up. "Thanks so much for the tea—and for the offer of your boat tomorrow, Phil. We'll be over at about eleven, then?"

Phil nodded. "I'll have the *Peggy Sue* all spruced up and ready to go," he said. "They have funerals at sea in Venice. I saw one once."

"So they do!" exclaimed Mum. "It is kind of romantic, somehow."

"Where are you parked?" asked Dad, always one to dispel a romantic atmosphere with tiresome practical details.

"The Island car park," said Mum.

"I'll walk to the car with you, Mum," said Jess.

Mum said her goodbyes—even, in quite a friendly way, to Fred. She and Dad exchanged a peck on the cheek. Phil actually gave her a hug, from which she emerged flushed and looking confused but sort of pleased. And then they went to the door.

The men stood at the door and waved as Jess and her mum set off down the narrow lane. Jess felt a throb of terror and braced herself for the steam, the snakes, the burning sparks of rage. But her mum said nothing. All she did was take Jess's arm, and they set off towards the Island car park.

"Mum," said Jess, "you're not cross, are you?"

"Cross?" said Mum, in rather a startled way. "No. Why should I be cross? I was feeling a bit guilty, actually."

"Guilty?" repeated Jess, amazed. "Why should you feel guilty?"

"Because I didn't manage to tell you about Dad," said Mum, with a sigh. "I should have said something long ago."

"Yeah, why didn't you?" asked Jess. "Not that I'm cross or upset or anything. It just would have been so much easier for us—and Dad too—if I'd known."

"We should have managed it better," said Mum. "Dad and I kept discussing it. I wasn't sure when you'd be old enough to accept it. I kept meaning to tell you, but somehow, the right moment never came. I did try, just a few days ago, when we went to see Lawrence of Arabia's cottage, and I tried again in that park in Penzance, but I'm afraid I lost my nerve."

"Well, it's OK now," said Jess. "There's no need to worry about that anymore."

"I thought you might freak out," said Mum.

"Well, I did, for a while, just at first," said Jess. "But I'm thrilled about it now. It is so much better than if he had got a girlfriend and a horrible baby and stuff. That would be dire. Instead, he's gay! That's so cool! Just wait till I tell all my friends! They'll be so envious!"

"Good. That's all right then," said Mum. She heaved a great sigh, as if a huge weight had been lifted from her shoulders.

"Are you sure you're not cross about—about Fred?" asked Jess, her heart pounding. "I really didn't know he was going to be here. It was a total surprise."

"It seems rather a flamboyant gesture on his part," said

Mum. Jess was glad they were walking side by side and she didn't have to look her mum in the eye at this crucial moment.

"Yes, well, Fred is a bit flamboyant," said Jess.

"He's trying to impress you?" said Mum.

"It's just his way," said Jess. Her heart was working up to a terrifying crescendo of thumping. She was sure it could be heard, like distant drumming, all over Cornwall. "Fred's, well, in some faintly ludicrous sort of way, Fred's actually—what might be known as my boyfriend, I suppose."

"I thought as much," said Mum. "I wasn't born yesterday."

There was a mesmerizing pause. They went on walking towards the car park. Jess braced herself for her mum's furious denunciation of Fred and all his satanic ways.

"Oh well," said her mum. *"C'est la vie."* And she shrugged, quite pleasantly.

"C'est what?" gasped Jess. Why, at this desperate moment, did her mum have to launch into French, of all things?

"That's life!" said Mum. *"Que será, será*—what will be, will be. And that's Spanish, by the way."

"Are you trying to tell me, in several different European languages, that you don't mind?" asked Jess.

"I'm saying that this moment was bound to come, and as I'm on holiday and in a rather good mood, I'm not going to let it bother me."

At this moment they arrived at the car, and as Mum turned to face Jess, she suddenly looked about ten years younger.

"I'm so glad you came," said Jess.

"So am I," said Mum. "I thought I'd do something impulsive, just for once. A spur-of-the-moment-type thing. And, well, you did need your PJs and stuff, so I did have a practical excuse. I hope I didn't ruin your evening, turning up out of the blue like that."

"Of course you didn't!" said Jess. "You made it just perfect!"

Jess threw her arms around her mum and hugged her harder than anyone has ever been hugged in the history of hugging. And her mum hugged her back, twice as hard as that.

Eventually the hug came to an end. They stood there in silence, looking at each other with tears in their eyes.

"You look pretty, Mum," said Jess.

"So do you, my babe," said Mum.

Then she got in the car, started it, and drove off with a funny little wave. Jess stood and watched her go. She looked so tiny, so vulnerable. Tears were running down Jess's cheeks now. "Please let her be safe," she whispered out loud. "Please let her be safe and happy forever and ever. And ever."

37

When Jess got back to Dad's house she found Phil and Fred in the kitchen. Dad was vacuuming. When she came in, he switched the vacuum off. They all looked at her.

"Was she cross?" asked Dad.

"No—it was strange, she was completely cool," said Jess.

"She must have been pissed off with me, though," said Fred.

"No. I told her you were my gentleman companion and she didn't bat an eyelid," said Jess. "I think Mum's had a really great evening and it's all sort of—well, sorted for her, now."

"Well, well," said Dad. "That's terrific. I thought she would be giving you a hard time."

"We'd got the stretcher ready," said Phil. "And the oxygen tent."

"I have to admit I thought she was going to eat me alive," said Jess. "But it just goes to show how surprising people can be."

"Well, I thought she was wonderful," said Phil.

"Her problem," said Jess, "is that she's never had any confidence in herself."

"That's because of me," said Dad.

"Now, Timbo!" said Phil sharply. "No wallowing in guilt! We agreed! You're only guilty on Thursdays between four and five!"

"Yes, Dad, don't be daft!" said Jess. "You and Mum split up ages ago. She's had years and years to get over it. She did go out with a few guys when I was younger, but there was nothing major. I'm sure she'll meet somebody nice one day. Somebody who suits her."

"She's very attractive, I think," said Phil. "Like our own dear Jess. Small, dark, and pixieish."

"At this point," said Fred, "Phil should reveal he has a brother who somehow never found the right woman. . . ."

"Yes!" said Dad. "A tall, tragic fisherman with steely gray eyes . . . I almost fancy him myself."

"God, I feel so guilty for not having a brother!" said Phil. "Or even a friend in need of a date."

"Maybe somebody who's looking after his elderly father," said Dad. "So Granny could have a hot date too."

"I don't think Granny would ever be interested in anybody else," said Jess. "Grandpa was the love of her life. She still adores him, you can tell." Again, somehow Jess caught Fred's eye. She was longing to be alone with him again. Just for the next sixty years.

"Maybe that's another reason your mum lacks confidence," said Phil thoughtfully. "I mean, if her parents' marriage was a terrific success."

Jess had never thought of that. Poor Mum! Of course. She must have felt even more of a sad unloved git, with Granny and Grandpa cuddling away flamboyantly for years and years, right under her nose.

"She just needs to get her confidence back," said Phil. "She's a really attractive woman. Don't you think, Timbo?"

"Well, I did marry her," Dad pointed out. "And considering I was gay, you have to conclude she must have been really something."

"I'd love to give her a makeover," said Phil. "With the right hair and clothes, and contact lenses, she could be a dead ringer for Ruby Wax."

"No, no," said Tim. "OK, she's small and dark. But Ruby Wax is such an extrovert, it's sort of the opposite of Madeleine, really."

"I think she looks like Jane Austen," said Fred.

"Fred!" cried Jess. "Brilliant, brilliant, brilliant! *Jackpot!*"

"What did Jane Austen look like?" asked Phil.

"Well, like Jess's mum," said Fred. "There's a picture of her on the cover of *Pride and Prejudice*."

"I didn't know you'd read *Pride and Prejudice*, Fred," said Jess, amazed and delighted.

"My mum's reading it, to be honest," said Fred. "But I don't have to read it. I saw the movie. And, of course, I *am* Mr. Darcy." And he tossed his head back and glared at her with what he imagined was aristocratic pride. Jess collapsed into giggles.

"Idiot!" she said. "You look like a dromedary!"

The long summer day drew to its close. They all went for a last walk on the beach. It was dark, and the surf crashed, ferocious and white, under the moon.

"OK," said Phil. "I'll be off now, to my mum's. I've got to get up early and get *Peggy Sue* ready for her special trip!" And he walked off past the Tate Gallery, waving. He hadn't kissed Dad goodbye or anything. So considerate.

"Right," said Dad when they got back in. "I'm going to make up a bed for Fred on the sofa. Whilst I'm doing that, why don't you two go and say goodnight up on the terrace, under the stars?"

"Oh God, Dad, must we?" sighed Jess. "We'd much rather stay down here and discuss literature."

"Well," said Fred, "we could go up and discuss astronomy."

"OK, then," said Jess as they trudged upstairs. "What's your favorite star?"

They walked out onto the deck. It was bathed in moonlight. Fred grabbed her and wrapped his long ape-like arms around her. "You are!" he whispered. "You're my favorite star. This has been the best day of my life." His heart was thudding away like mad. They sank into a long, long kiss. Then they came up for breath. "Apart from when Man United won the European Cup, of course," added Fred.

Jess beat him up slightly, and then decided to bury her nose in his neck instead. "You smell nice," said Jess. His skin, his hair, smelt kind of spicy. It wasn't aftershave or anything. It was Fred's very own special scent. She wondered if, when Granny and Grandpa had kissed under the moon, Grandpa's skin had been so delicious, all those long years ago.

Eventually they went in, and Jess kissed her dad goodnight,

and went to her own room. She loved her room. It was so plain and tidy, so blue and white. She pulled off all her clothes and threw them about. The room looked even better now. She unpacked the bag Mum had brought. There were pajamas, clean socks, pants, her favorite blue T-shirt for tomorrow, her sponge bag, tissues, and a lovely gift box from the Eden Project containing a foam bath, moisturizer, and other delectable goodies. "Mum!" she said aloud, "you are a legend!"

Jess switched on her mobile, and there was a message from Flora.

HI JSS! SRY IVE BN OUTA TCH. HVNG GR8 TM HRE. HV MET FAB BOY CLLD DAVE. TTL MORON, GRGS. HW'S YR DAD?

Hastily Jess composed a reply. AM AT DAD'S NOW. GUESS WHAT! HE'S GAY!!! I'VE MET HIS BOYFRIEND AND EVERY-THING! WE JUST HAD A GREAT DAY. EVEN MUM SEEMS RE-LAXED. A message came back right away. WHAAAAAAAT? YR DADS GAY!!!??? U LCKY THNG! WSH MY DD WS GAY. HES BORNG AS HLL.

Jess tapped away at her keypad again. FRED'S COME DOWN TO ST. IVES. AMAZING! IT WAS A TOTAL SUR-PRISE. HE HITCHED DOWN JUST TO SEE ME!

MST B LURVE came Flora's reply. GTTA GO NW—DAVES BY CMPFRE W8ING FR A SNOG. TXT U TMW. BG HGS, FLO XXX.

Jess sighed in satisfaction, switched off her mobile, and went to sleep. She hadn't felt so contented for years. But she still dreamed she was being chased through deserted streets by a man with a pizza instead of a face. She only just man-aged to escape him at the last minute by summoning all her strength and rising up into the air. Dreams are so weird.

ext day Mum arrived with Granny and the urn.
They had to wait at Dad's house until high tide,
apparently. Granny threw her arms around Dad
and told him she'd missed him. Dad looked pleased and offered her a freshly baked cheese scone.

"Where's this lovely Phil I've heard so much about?" said
Granny, looking round. Dad blushed.

"He's getting his boat ready," he explained.

They sat on the sofa together talking about Grandpa. Dad
and Grandpa had got on really well. Grandpa was seriously into DIY and Dad had once helped him build a shed
in his back garden. Dad had painted flowers all over it so it
blended in with the rose hedge, and as a joke he'd added a
cat's face looking out of the leaves.

Mum went up on the terrace with Jess and Fred. Jess

carried up a tray of tea. She had got used to Dad's kitchen now. It was nice, knowing where things were. As if she belonged here. She didn't want *just* to belong here. But she wanted to belong here *as well*.

"Dad's house is so lovely," sighed Mum, as Jess put down the tray. "This deck—the view over the roofs . . ."

"Our house is lovely too, Mum," said Jess.

"Is it?" asked Mum, looking anxious. "Do you really think so? It's a mess, most of the time."

"Well, that's because we're not as tidy as Dad," said Jess. "But we could paint our sitting room blue and white if you like."

"Yes, maybe we should," said Mum. "It really needs redecorating. But I've been putting it off because I hate trying to reach up to the ceiling."

"I'll come and give you a hand if you like," said Fred. "I have these long arms: may as well use them."

"Oh, will you really, Fred?" said Jess's mum. "How kind of you! That would be marvelous!" Mum's eyes shone, and then she seemed a bit embarrassed, and started fussing with the tea tray. She took the lid off the teapot and stirred the tea.

"Leave that teapot alone!" said Jess playfully. "You relax, for once. I'm going to be Mother." Jess poured the tea out and passed the scones round.

They sipped their tea and ate Dad's delicious scones. Nobody said anything very much. It was just peaceful and relaxed. The sun grew hot, but they were protected by a sort of awning thing that Dad had rigged up.

The last scone sat tempting on the plate, sending its waves of hot cheese tantalizingly through the air.

"You have it, Mum!" said Jess.

"No, you have it, Fred!" said Mum.

"No, no, you have it!" said Fred.

"Aren't we all polite?" said Jess. "But I happen to know there are loads more scones down in the kitchen."

"I'll go and get a couple more," said Fred. He got up and clattered down the stairs.

Mum yawned, stretched as if she was very relaxed, and ran her fingers through her hair. All the wiry anxiety seemed to have gone out of her.

"How's Flora?" she asked.

"OK," said Jess. "She's fine."

"Oh, good," said Mum. "Such a nice girl."

"I think part of my problem with Flora," said Jess, "is I've always been a bit jealous. It is tough, having a friend who looks like a goddess."

"Rubbish!" said Mum. "OK, she is beautiful, but so are you in your way."

"In *our* way," said Jess. "I look just like you, Mum. And guess what Fred said last night?"

Her mum looked a bit tense for a moment, in case Jess was about to reveal Fred's declaration of love, or offer of immediate marriage.

"What did he say?" she asked.

"He said you looked just like Jane Austen!" said Jess—in a rather furtive whisper, because she could hear Fred coming back upstairs with the cheese scones.

"Jane *Austen*?" mouthed her mum in amazement, as if she might have misheard, and Fred might really have said she resembled Jane Mostyn, or Shane Frosting, or something. Jess nodded.

Fred came out onto the deck, and offered Jess's mum a cheese scone. She took one.

"Oh, thank you, Fred!" she said. "You're an absolute angel!" And she gave him an utterly dazzling smile.

Fred looked startled. When he'd made that Jane Austen comment, he'd really struck gold. If you ever want to sweep a middle-aged librarian off her feet, tell her that she looks just like Jane Austen. Jess could tell, by the way her mum looked at Fred, she would adore him forever. Well, they could adore him in stereo.

When it was high tide, they all walked down to the harbor. Dad was carrying the urn. They walked right down onto the pier. Phil's boat was waiting at the bottom of a flight of stone steps that went down to the sea. He was dressed all in white, and the boat was decorated with white flowers.

"Oh my goodness!" said Granny. "How beautiful! It takes my breath away!"

Dad and Mum helped Granny get into the boat. Phil held her hand, steadied her, made her comfortable and helped her into a cute little life jacket. It had been decided that Granny would go out on her own with Phil. That was the way she wanted it.

Phil fixed Grandpa's urn safely to the prow of the boat, and decorated it with flowers and white ribbons. Then he started up the engine. Granny held on to the side of the boat, looked up, and waved with a happy smile, as if she was going on a pleasure jaunt.

Phil gave a sort of salute, and steered the boat out of the harbor. Off it went, out into the bay. The sea was as placid as a pane of glass. They stood on the pier and watched for a minute. Mum got her hankie out and wiped her eyes. Dad gently put his arm round her shoulders.

Jess liked seeing her parents close and sharing a tender moment. But she realized that she was free forever from that nagging desire that she'd always had at the back of her mind: that they should get together again. It was impossible. You could as soon marry a budgie and a haddock.

Fred stood close to her. He didn't put his arm round her, but their arms touched as they leaned on the wall of the pier. Jess could feel Fred's warmth. It was glorious. Thank God he was not a reptile. Jess felt very sorry for cold-blooded crocodiles, for a moment. It must be hell, trying to have a relationship without any cozy hugs.

They watched the little boat as it went out into the very center of the bay and then stopped. It was too far away to see what was happening, but there was a brief pause. Seagulls called, the sun danced on the waves. Jess was secretly relieved she hadn't had to go out in the boat. She had been terrified she might ruin the whole thing by puking in Technicolor all over Phil's white trousers.

After a while, the boat came back again. As it got closer, they could see that Granny had a flower in her hair. Jess smiled to herself.

They all crowded down the steps and helped Granny out again. Her eyes were a little bit wet, but her smile was bright.

"We saw a dolphin," said Granny. "It reminded me of Grandpa, somehow. The smile, you know."

"I've had an idea," said Dad. "As soon as I get back to my studio, I'm going to start work on a painting of Grandpa. Sitting at the door of his shed, just like he used to do."

"When he wanted to escape from my nagging," said Granny. "What a lovely idea! Paint him in that old green tweed jacket, Tim. That was his favorite."

"So, anyone for funeral fish and chips?" asked Phil. "Take 'em home and guzzle 'em with a bottle of cold champagne?"

"Oh yes, please!" said Mum. "Just perfect!"

After lunch, it seemed the grown-ups no longer needed any support or counseling. Phil went back to work. Mum lay on a lounger in the shade on Dad's terrace, and closed her eyes. Granny and Dad went through an old photo album looking for photos of Grandpa, to help Dad prepare for the painting he was going to do.

"Come on," whispered Fred, "let's go to the beach!"

"Yes! Let's swim!" said Jess. "Though you must promise not to stare in dismay at my podge when you see me in my bikini!"

"And you must avert your gaze from my puny sticklike legs," said Fred. "It'll only be a matter of time before a bodybuilder comes up and kicks sand in my face."

Jess grabbed her swimming kit and a couple of beach

towels. Mum made them promise they would rub SPF 30 on each other.

"Oh, *Mum!*" sighed Jess as if the very idea was boring as hell. Although of course she was looking forward to rubbing sun cream on Fred as much as a cat looks forward to cornering a sardine under the kitchen table.

They went out. The sun was bouncing up and down the street as if it had been ordered as part of a Sun, Surf 'n' Lurve Holiday Romance Package.

"God!" said Jess. "I'm so happy it's absolutely revolting! I expect some scaffolding will collapse onto us, or something."

"Or maybe we'll get run over," said Fred. "Being very happy is just asking for trouble." He grabbed her hand and squeezed it so hard, it made her knuckles crack. This was the best day of her life so far—even with several broken fingers.

The beach, though crowded, was immense, and they soon found a semiprivate corner only a few yards away from three bickering families and some clinically obese people playing badminton. It was heaven on earth.

"Right," said Jess. "I'm going to the loos to change into my bikini."

"I'll stay here," said Fred. "I've got my swimmers on under my jeans." And he ripped off his jeans and revealed a very long pair of quite stylish gray shorts. "I'm not taking my T-shirt off yet," he said. "I hate my nipples and when you see them it will be all over between us."

"You should learn to love them, Fred," said Jess. "Give them names. Treat them as pets. It worked for me."

Fred grinned, laid out the beach towels side by side, and

lowered himself gently into a relaxing horizontal position.

"Hurry up!" he said. "And you might as well get us a couple of ice creams while you're there. Anything with chocolate and peanuts will do for me."

Jess set off for the rather distant loos. St. Ives had four beaches, and Dad had said this one was best for swimming. It backed onto a steep hillside covered with trees. It was about as scenic as anywhere could be without actual coconut palms, and added to Jess's mood of crazy joy.

Even the loos seemed touched with divinity. The faint smell of disinfectant would be forever etched in her memory as the most delightful whiff. She might even buy some and squirt it on her pulse points for all future hot dates. She crammed herself into her bikini. It was a mistake, of course: yellow with blue polka dots. But at least it covered most of her bum. Would Fred find it ludicrously old-fashioned that she hadn't got a gold lamé Brazilian thong? Too bad. Her buttocks must never be revealed to the general public.

Jess had established once, with the aid of two big mirrors, that her bottom looked like two bald men whispering to each other. This misfortune could only be disguised with a tattoo of the map of the world, with the Americas on one buttock and Africa on the other. Until Jess had saved up enough for the tattoo, the thong would have to wait.

She stuffed her clothes into her shoulder bag, slipped into her flip-flops, and ventured out of the loo, feeling very embarrassed. There were three women queuing and they glared at her for keeping them waiting.

"Sorry," she murmured, and rushed outside. The sunlight felt good on her bare flesh, but she knew she only had a few minutes before she would begin to burn. She had to get back to Fred and force him to rub on the SPF 30. But first she must get the ice creams.

The ice cream seller didn't have anything with peanuts and chocolate, so Jess bought two enormous cones with a towering, fluffy pyramid of whipped ice cream leaning dangerously out of each. Then she squinted into the bright glare of the beach to find Fred again.

He wasn't there. He *wasn't there*! Jess's heart leapt. Her eyes raked the beach. He wasn't where she'd left him. There was a couple talking where she thought he would be. *Wait, don't panic*, thought Jess, licking both ice cream cones urgently as they were already wilting under the hot sun. *Maybe he's just gone for a swim*.

She scanned the people in the sea. They were just bobbing heads, but none of them looked like Fred. Oh my God! He'd drowned! Just minutes ago she'd felt it was the happiest day of her life, and now, suddenly, she had plunged right back into absolute torture.

Jess advanced down towards the beach, still holding the two ice cream cones, and still licking them now and then even though she was already planning what to wear for Fred's funeral. She would go back to their beach towels. Maybe somebody had seen him. There was a couple nearby, the guy sitting on his towel, the girl standing up, talking. She would ask them.

Wait! Jess looked at the couple again. The guy wasn't just anybody—it was Fred! *Fred!* Fred sitting on the beach talking to a girl! A slim blond girl, of course, tanned and—unless Jess's eyes deceived her, wearing a gold lamé Brazilian thong. She was flashing her gorgeous pert little body at him, the bitch! Her golden thighs were six inches away from Fred's hypnotized face!

What the hell was he playing at? She would kill him for this! She would kill the girl as well—even more sadistically! In the time it took her to slip into a bikini, Fred had slipped into a whole new relationship! Jess marched furiously down towards them. Fred had taken his T-shirt off. So the blonde in the thong had been allowed to see his nipples before her! What an insult! This was so *completely* the worst day of her life!

*F*or a moment Jess wondered if the girl might somehow be Flora—crazy, she knew Flora was at Riverdene, but your mind plays strange tricks when you are plummeting from cloud nine down towards the blackest pits of hell.

As she got nearer to them, Fred looked round guiltily, caught her eye, and pulled a weird, embarrassed sort of face.

"Hi, Jess!" he called. The beautiful blonde looked across at her and smiled. It was one of those catty, insincere smiles that hide a wicked desire to truss you up, fling you off a cliff, and run off to Acapulco with your helpless boyfriend.

"Well, I must dash!" said the girl, and suddenly slapped both her buttocks playfully as if to draw attention to their splendor. "Shall I go for a swim or not? What do you think?" She turned round and looked at the sea—to show Fred her ass, obviously.

"Oh, go for it," said Fred, rather urgently.

"OK! Here goes! My mum was breaststroke champion of Swindon, so I suppose I should make an effort!" And she ran off, her cute little bottom wobbling tauntingly all the way to the waves.

"I hope she drowns!" said Jess. "For God's sake! I can't leave you unattended for a split second! All I did was go and get an ice cream and when I come back you're chatting up some flashy tart in a thong!"

"I was *not* chatting her up!" said Fred, scrambling to his feet. "She just came over and hit on me! I can't help it if other women find me irresistible!" He was grinning, the pig! He thought it was some big joke!

A wave of red-hot fire surged through Jess's veins. She couldn't help it. Her whole body shook with jealous rage. In an instant perfect happiness had been replaced by sheer hell. Fred had been chatted up while her back was turned—and he thought it was a laugh!

Giving in to a moment of sheer weird madness, Jess plunged both ice cream cones onto Fred's chest—one on each nipple. For an instant they sort of stuck to him, looking like the pointy bra Madonna once wore, and then they fell off, streaking melted ice cream down his shorts and his legs. The cones fell into the sand, and became tragic and ruined.

"You idiot!" said Fred, looking deeply embarrassed. "I was looking forward to that!"

"Well, if you want it, you can lick it off your nipples!"

growled Jess. "Or maybe your glamorous new friend can lick it off for you!"

Suddenly Jess became aware that some of the families nearby were sniggering. *Oh my God,* she thought, *I look a complete prat!* For an instant she was frozen in total horror. She felt a dozen pairs of eyes on her. She was suddenly the biggest idiot on the beach. There was no way out of this mega-humiliation.

No, wait! There *was* a way out. Jess reached desperately, blindly, for her old friend, her guardian angel: comedy.

"It's just not good enough, Quentin!" she bawled, her voice gradually becoming more and more ridiculously upper-class. "I can't trust you anywhere! There was that croupier in Las Vegas—what was she called? Rosie. Such a ludicrous nose—and *not* a natural blonde.

"Then there was that milkmaid in Switzerland. What a fat cow! And the milkmaid was a tad overweight too."

There was a ripple of laughter from families nearby. Fred's face—Fred's darling face—cleared, and the horrible look of embarrassment gave way to his usual witty grin.

"I only asked if I could squeeze her udders!" he protested. There was more laughter from their audience. What a crude lot this bunch were. Trust Fred to appeal to their baser instincts.

"It's no use! I've had it up to here with you and your floozies!" said Jess. "When we get back home you're going back in your box!"

"No! No! Not the box!" pleaded Fred.

"Yes! Six months in the box, and then you'll only be allowed out to go to church! With a paper bag over your head!"

"OK, OK! Mind you, that lady vicar is a good-looking gal. I think a dog collar does something for a woman. Or are they called bitch collars if the vicar's a lady?"

"Quentin, you're an animal!" roared Jess. "Jeeves, my horsewhip! You've gone too far, and you're going to get a hiding!"

Fred gave a terrified yell and ran off towards the sea. Jess followed, brandishing an imaginary whip. And behind them, just for a moment, she thought she could hear people *applauding*.

But she didn't look round. She just plunged into the sea and chased Fred, who was swimming off with madly flailing arms. Jess easily caught up with him, grabbed him and ducked his head underwater. Fred dived down, escaped her, and bobbed up a couple of yards away. Jess attacked him again, laughing, but he grabbed both her arms and wouldn't let go. He was surprisingly strong for a thin bloke who lay on the sofa for most of his leisure hours.

"I thought that went rather well," said Fred. "But maybe we should save up the ice cream hurling for the end. In fact, next time I think you should hit me in the face with a whole custard pie."

"Fred, your approach to comedy is so crude!" said Jess. "That gag about udders too. I prefer sophisticated one-liners."

"Yeah, but they loved it," said Fred. "A seaside audience is always a bit coarse. And so am I!"

He grabbed her leg under water. Jess kicked him away, laughing. She was so relieved. Everything was OK again.

Though she could still see the blond girl over Fred's shoulder. She had swum off about a hundred yards and was talking, possibly about breaststroke, to a hairy-chested man lying on a surfboard with a chain round his neck.

How totally stupid I was to lose it like that, thought Jess. Her jealousy had nearly ruined everything.

"I love it when you're jealous!" said Fred mischievously.

"I wasn't really jealous!" said Jess.

"Yes you were—your face went red."

"That was just good acting."

"How disappointing!" said Fred. "I was jealous as hell, myself. You and that damned ice cream man getting all lovey-dovey over the whipped cream cones."

"Fred! He was a hundred years old and bald with no teeth!"

Fred grabbed her feet and started to tickle. Jess plunged and screamed with laughter.

"Not fair! Not fair!" she gasped, swallowing water and coughing. "Stop! Stop!"

"I won't stop until you apologize for getting cross!" said Fred. "And wasting the ice creams."

"Well, what hope is there for me, with blond bombshells like her taking a fancy to you? And that girl at the caterer's—Rosie," said Jess.

"Blondes are not my type," said Fred. "I prefer a horrid little dark podgy girl! Especially when she's angry! And by the way, Rosie was a complete invention."

"So you even go out of your way to make me jealous!" said Jess, splashing water in his face.

"I can't help it!" spluttered Fred. "You're magnificent when you're angry! Hey! This was our first row. Wasn't it great? I can't wait till the next one."

And he put his arms round her and kissed her with magnificent panache, whilst cleverly avoiding drowning. This was quite an achievement, considering that neither of them had parents who were breaststroke champions.

"I'm sorry I was jealous," said Jess after the kiss. "But I quite like this making-up bit." Jess had to accept it: there would always be gorgeous blond girls hovering when her back was turned. Girls with tanned faces and hair bleached by the sun. Granny had been right about the beach being a dangerous place.

She just had to hope and pray that Fred persisted in his weird, perverted preference for her rather grotesque pallid self. And oh God! She had to slosh on the SPF 30 as soon as they got out of the sea. Red was so *not* her favorite color. Especially for noses and shoulders.

They swam out beyond the breakwater and let themselves be lifted up by the ocean swell.

"Oh my God!" said Jess. "I'm totally out of my depth!"

"It's perfectly safe," said Fred, "just lie on your back and imagine you're a dolphin!"

Fred grabbed her legs and whirled her round and round in the water. Jess lay back and felt the sky wheel above her, and the sea whirl all around her, until it all became a blur, just a single, glorious blue.

About the Author

Sue Limb lives on an organic farm in a remote part of Gloucestershire. Her writing career has included various assignments for magazines and newspapers, radio work, television series, and several novels for adults published in Britain. Her books for children include *Big and Little, China Lee, Me Jane, Big Trouble, Mr. Loopy and Mrs. Snoopy*, and *Come Back, Grandma*, which was short-listed for the Smarties Prize. Sue's first novel about the charmingly crazed Jess Jordan, *Girl, 15, Charming but Insane*, is available from Delacorte Press.

Sue Limb is quite interested in gardening, travel, green politics, agriculture, and especially rare breeds of poultry, about which she is particularly mad.

GIRL, NEARLY 16
ABSOLUTE TORTURE

A READERS GUIDE

Sue Limb

1. On page 54, Limb writes: "It would be so, so cool if Mum knew about Fred and approved and everything. It was just that Mum had often been kind of hard on men, and Jess hadn't quite managed to pluck up her courage and mention the subject." What do you think about Jess's decision to keep her romance with Fred from her mother? Do you think her mum is actually anti-men enough to disapprove of Jess and Fred's relationship?

2. Much confusion arises from Fred's vaguely worded text messages. Look at two of the messages he sends Jess during her vacation: he describes his coworkers as "ALL GIRLS. KIND OF LOW-CALORIE SUGABABES" (page 49) and sends the message "DISASTER. MANAGED TO DROP A BIG DISH OF CRÈME CARAMEL ALL DOWN CHARLOTTE'S CLEAVAGE" (page 58). Do you think Fred is trying to incite Jess's jealousy, or is the brevity of the text messaging format making things sound more scandalous than they really are?

3. During her vacation, Jess strongly suspects that her best friend, Flora, may be conspiring to spend time alone with Fred. Do you think Jess's suspicion of her best friend is warranted? Do you think it says something about the state of their friendship, or does it have more to do with Jess's personality?

4. On page 94, Jess asks her mother, "If you could date a writer, any writer, who would it be?" What would your answer to this question be, and why?

5. On page 100, after recalling an instance when she felt jealous of a woman who'd gotten Grandpa's attention, Granny tells Jess, "Always remember, dear, the beach can be a dangerous place. What with everyone taking their clothes off and throwing caution to the winds." Do you agree with this assessment? Are some locations or situations more likely than others to make you feel jealous?

6. On page 118, Jess's mom begins to confide in her daughter about what went wrong between her and Jess's dad. She starts to cry, commenting that she believes Jess's dad stopped feeling attracted to her, and Jess responds with a joke. On page 120, Limb writes of Jess's mom's reaction: "For a moment she looked a bit cross that her tragic moment had been railroaded into comedy." What do you think of this response? Are there some situations in which joking is inappropriate? Do you think Jess's constant joking is a character flaw, or a desirable talent?

7. Jess's family engages in a good deal of deception in this book: Jess's mom avoids telling her about her father's homosexuality, Jess hides her relationship with Fred from both parents, and Jess's father tries to pass Phil off as a visiting friend. Do you think all these lies imply an inability to deal with the truth? Do you think Jess and her parents will be more open with each other in the future? If so, why?

8. When Jess is told of her father's homosexuality, her reaction is "It's brilliant! It's so cool! Wait till I tell all

3

my friends! They'll be *so* jealous!" (page 162). Do you think this is a believable reaction for a modern teenager? Do you think it's the reaction Jess's parents were expecting?

9. On page 181, when Jess's mum shows up at her dad's house, Jess ponders, "Now, at the very moment when Jess had finally got together with Dad, and understood what he was all about, and was having the wildest, the most wonderful time, now her mum had to turn up. Hammering on the door like the vice squad or something. Ruining everything." But just a few moments later, on page 183, Limb writes, "Suddenly Jess felt a wave of tenderness for her mum. . . . She looked small and sad and real. And tired." What do you think Jess has realized about her mother that accounts for this change in the way she sees her mum? Which image do you think is more accurate?

10. On page 212, Jess confronts Fred about his flirtation with the bikinied blonde and soon makes things awkward between them. She chooses to make a joke out of the whole interaction, and Fred cheerfully plays along. What do you make of this method of conflict resolution? What are some other ways Jess might have handled the situation? Do you think the issue is resolved, or will Jess's jealousy come up again?

IN HER OWN WORDS

A conversation with

Sue Limb

Q: *Girl, 15, Charming but Insane* and *Girl, (Nearly) 16: Absolute Torture* both chronicle the charmingly insane life of Jess Jordan, and you've written a third novel, *Girl, (Going on) 17: Pants on Fire.* Did you conceive of Jess's story as a trilogy, or did you write one book and then find yourself eager to revisit the character?

A: I enjoyed the first book so much that I wanted to spend more time with Jess. I didn't conceive of it as a trilogy—in fact, I'm writing a fourth book right now. I don't think so far ahead. The books sort of evolve rather than being fully planned before I start. I could go back and spend time with Jess again and again. Knowing the characters well is a real advantage.

Q: In *Girl, (Nearly) 16,* Jess deals pretty heavily with jealousy. What do you think of Jess's jealous behavior in this book? Is it typical first-love stuff, or totally over the top?

A: Jealousy is just one of those horrible emotions which we all suffer from, and we hate ourselves even as we're feeling it. It feeds on being apart from your boyfriend and not knowing what he's up to. It's a kind of fantasy. I think jealousy is a biological phenomenon. You see it in the animal world all the time, with creatures competing for mates. And comedy evolves so easily from strong negative emotions that jealousy provides a rich vein of laughs.

Q: Jess and her family don't necessarily lie to each other in this book—they do a *little* of that—but mostly, they seem to omit important information when talking to each other. Jess avoids telling her parents about Fred, and Jess's parents avoid telling her the truth about why they split up. But when everything comes out at the end, it works out surprisingly well. Why do you think they misread each other so? It seems as if they're all waiting for a terrible reaction that never quite comes.

A: British people are often more buttoned up or shy or reserved than our American cousins. We avoid embarrassment and we don't feel easy with lavish displays of emotion. This is one reason we Brits are famous for our comedy—because uneasiness always creates amusing situations. If Jess and her family communicated freely and easily with one another, there would be no story. I always tell creative writing students, "Give your characters problems and create misunderstandings." Without that there would be no comedy and no drama either.

Q: Jess seems dismayed early on to think that her mother is fairly anti-men, but when they're on the road trip, she's equally dismayed by her mother's flirtations. Which do you think is scarier for Jess: the idea that her mother might remain alone, or that she may start dating again?

A: Any girl would feel sad to think that her mum might be alone for the rest of her life, and getting older. It would also make it harder for the girl to leave home eventually—seeing her mum as isolated and lonely and feeling responsible for her happiness. However, though she might want her mum to have a boyfriend again one day, Jess doesn't actually want to watch the process! (It is gross to see your mum flirting. Or even worse,

7

dancing!) Mums should always behave with decorum in public. I always do. (Apart from an isolated incident with a limbo dancer and a pint of fruit punch . . .) Otherwise, major embarrassment can result.

Q: Jess seems to truly believe at one point in this book that Fred and Flora might betray her by getting together while she's away. Do you think Jess is completely out of her mind with jealousy here? Or is she picking up on something in Flora, a character who's used to having things her way?

A: Jess is also remembering that Flora admitted quite recently that she had a crush on Fred. Also, Flora is really beautiful. I think girls with beautiful friends are always on edge when their boyfriends are in the company of the beauteous one. It's a natural reaction, though very primitive (one might almost say biological).

Q: Jess reacts to the news of her dad's homosexuality quite well—she's excited and enthusiastic, not at all upset. Do you think her reaction stems from her fairly cheerful personality, or is it typical of her generation?

A: I hope this is the reaction most modern teenagers would produce, because homophobia is an ugly and negative phenomenon. Gay life and gay style are usually perceived as cool in the UK. I guess her parents were more on edge about her reaction, though.

Q: Granny is usually a fairly happy character, but she has a hard time letting go of Grandpa. Why do you think scattering his ashes is harder for her than she anticipated?

A: It's the difficulty of letting go. The ashes are all she has left in the physical world of the man she spent her life loving. I suppose she found that his mortal remains meant more to her than she had anticipated.

Q: **Several times in *Girl, (Nearly) 16,* Jess defuses emotional or awkward moments with comedy. Do you think she ever uses comedy as a defense, to keep people from getting too close?**

A: Comedy is often used to keep people at arm's length— even people one really loves. Americans are much less embarrassed about saying "I love you!" and hugging their loved ones in public. We Brits still sometimes find this a bit difficult, not to say tacky. Any kind of awkward emotion—embarrassment, anxiety, fear—can be turned into a joke by using irony. If you're in tune with this approach, you can find it just as loving but more bracing, not quite so slushy and needy. Jess is afraid of sounding needy. (Possibly because she is!) It's a great breakthrough for Jess and her mum when they finally share a hug and express their love for each other.

Q: **During the scene where her mum comes to drop off her overnight bag, Jess seems to reach an understanding about her mother. Do you think Jess favors one parent over the other? Is Jess's personality closer to her father's or her mother's?**

A: Jess has grown up with her mother but still sees her in a different light when they are away from home. She sees her partly through other people's eyes, perhaps for the first time. Because she's a single parent, Jess's mum has had to be strict with Jess. She has not felt free to relax

9

and joke as much as Jess's dad does. Jess's dad, being a glamorous visitor rather than part of the furniture, can enjoy a more charismatic and less responsible role.

I think Jess's character is a mixture of the two, though the more immediate resemblance is to her witty and wisecracking dad. However, physically she looks a lot more like her mum: small and dark.

Q: When Jess and Fred are on the beach, he admits that he made up the Rosie character, and that he was trying to make Jess jealous. But later, he seems totally put off by her jealous rampage when she attacks him with the ice cream. Is Fred a hypocrite? Or did he not realize the depths of jealousy to which Jess would sink? Or was he just really, really hungry?

A: I think Fred often gives way to what seems the most entertaining impulse and sometimes doesn't realize its implications. He is startled on the beach because she attacks him in public, I suppose. Fred's not terribly good at "joined-up" emotional intelligence. Well, boys usually do develop more slowly than girls. At the beginning of the third book, *Girl, (Going on) 17: Pants on Fire*, Fred does something totally astonishing, entirely on impulse, without realizing the implications of his actions. He's adorable, but he's still got a lot of growing up to do!

Q: What's next for Jess and her charmingly insane gang?

A: Buy *Girl, (Going on) 17: Pants on Fire* when it comes out and you'll find out! All I can say is there are several agonizingly embarrassing episodes involving underwear, and Jess also gets into the worst trouble in school that she has ever endured. . . .

RELATED TITLES

Girl, 15, Charming but Insane • Sue Limb
978-0-385-73215-4
With her hilariously active imagination, Jess Jordan has a tendency to complicate her life, but now, as she's finally getting closer to her crush, she's determined to keep things under control. Readers will fall in love with Sue Limb's insanely optimistic heroine.

The Unlikely Romance of Kate Bjorkman
Louise Plummer
978-0-375-89521-0
I'm Kate Bjorkman. I don't like romance novels. They're full of three-paragraph kisses describing people's tongues and spittle. But I wrote this romance novel about myself, using *The Romance Writer's Phrase Book*. This is the honest truth, and I want truth even in romance. I'm betting you'll want the same.

The Sisterhood of the Traveling Pants • Ann Brashares
978-0-385-73058-7
Over a few bags of cheese puffs, four girls decide to form a sisterhood and take the vow of the Sisterhood of the Traveling Pants. The next morning, they say goodbye. And then the journey of the Pants, and the most memorable summer of their lives, begin.

Stargirl • Jerry Spinelli
978-0-440-41677-7
Stargirl. From the day she arrives at quiet Mica High in a burst of color and sound, the hallways hum with the murmur of "Stargirl, Stargirl." The students are enchanted. Then they turn on her.

A Great and Terrible Beauty • Libba Bray
978-0-385-73231-4
Sixteen-year-old Gemma Doyle is sent to the Spence Academy in London after tragedy strikes her family in India. Lonely, guilt-ridden, and prone to visions of the future that have an uncomfortable habit of coming true, Gemma finds her reception a chilly one. But at Spence, Gemma's power to attract the supernatural unfolds; she becomes entangled with the school's most powerful girls and discovers her mother's connection to a shadowy group called the Order. A curl-up-under-the-covers Victorian gothic.

11

Counting Stars • David Almond • 978-0-440-41826-9
With stories that shimmer and vibrate in the bright heat of memory, David Almond creates a glowing mosaic of his life growing up in a large, loving Catholic family in northeastern England.

Before We Were Free • Julia Alvarez • 978-0-440-23784-6
Under a dictatorship in the Dominican Republic in 1960, young Anita lives through a fight for freedom that changes her world forever.

The Chocolate War • Robert Cormier • 978-0-375-82987-1
Jerry Renault dares to disturb the universe in this groundbreaking and now classic novel, an unflinching portrait of corruption and cruelty in a boys' prep school.

Dr. Franklin's Island • Ann Halam • 978-0-440-23781-5
A plane crash leaves Semi, Miranda, and Arnie stranded on a tropical island, totally alone. Or so they think. Dr. Franklin is a mad scientist who has set up his laboratory on the island, and the three teens are perfect subjects for his frightening experiments in genetic engineering.

Keeper of the Night • Kimberly Willis Holt • 978-0-553-49441-9
Living on the island of Guam, a place lush with memories and tradition, young Isabel struggles to protect her family and cope with growing up after her mother's suicide.

When Zachary Beaver Came to Town • Kimberly Willis Holt • 978-0-440-23841-6
Toby's small, sleepy Texas town is about to get a jolt with the arrival of Zachary Beaver, billed as the fattest boy in the world. Toby is in for a summer unlike any other—a summer sure to change his life.

The Parallel Universe of Liars • Kathleen Jeffrie Johnson • 978-0-440-23852-2
Surrounded by superficiality, infidelity, and lies, Robin, a self-

READERS CIRCLE BOOKS

described chunk, isn't sure what to make of her hunky neighbor's sexual advances, or of the attention paid her by a new boy in town who seems to notice more than her body.

Ghost Boy • Iain Lawrence • 978-0-440-41668-5
Fourteen-year-old Harold Kline is an albino—an outcast. When the circus comes to town, Harold runs off to join it in hopes of discovering who he is and what he wants in life. Is he a circus freak or just a normal guy?

The Lightkeeper's Daughter • Iain Lawrence • 978-0-385-73127-0
Imagine growing up on a tiny island with no one but your family. For Squid McCrae, returning to the island after three years away unleashes a storm of bittersweet memories, revelations, and accusations surrounding her brother's death.

Gathering Blue • Lois Lowry • 978-0-440-22949-0
Lamed and suddenly orphaned, Kira is mysteriously taken to live in the palatial Council Edifice, where she is expected to use her gifts as a weaver to do the bidding of the all-powerful Guardians.

The Giver • Lois Lowry • 978-0-440-23768-6
Jonas's world is perfect. Everything is under control. There is no war or fear or pain. There are no choices, until Jonas is given an opportunity that will change his world forever.

Shades of Simon Gray • Joyce McDonald • 978-0-440-22804-2
Simon is the ideal teenager—smart, reliable, hardworking, trustworthy. Or is he? After Simon's car crashes into a tree and he slips into a coma, another portrait of him begins to emerge.

Zipped • Laura and Tom McNeal • 978-0-375-83098-3
In a suspenseful novel of betrayal, forgiveness, and first love, fifteen-year-old Mick Nichols opens an e-mail he was never meant to see—and learns a terrible secret.

Harmony • Rita Murphy • 978-0-440-22923-0
Power is coursing through Harmony—the power to affect the

13

universe with her energy. This is a frightening gift for a girl who
has always hated being different, and Harmony must decide
whether to hide her abilities or embrace the consequences—good
and bad—of her full strength.

Cuba 15 • Nancy Osa • 978-0-385-73233-8
Violet Paz's upcoming *quinceañero*, a girl's traditional fifteenth-
birthday coming-of-age ceremony, awakens her interest in her
Cuban roots—and sparks a fire of conflicting feelings about Cuba
within her family.

Both Sides Now • Ruth Pennebaker • 978-0-440-22933-9
A compelling look at breast cancer through the eyes of a mother
and daughter. Liza must learn a few life lessons from her mother,
Rebecca, about the power of family.

Her Father's Daughter • Mollie Poupeney • 978-0-440-22879-0
As she matures from a feisty tomboy of seven to a spirited young
woman of fourteen, Maggie discovers that the only constant in her
life of endless new homes and new faces is her ever-emerging
sense of herself.

Pool Boy • Michael Simmons • 978-0-385-73196-6
Brett Gerson is the kind of guy you love to hate—until his father is
thrown in prison and Brett has to give up the good life. That's when
some swimming pools enter his world and change everything.

Milkweed • Jerry Spinelli • 978-0-440-42005-7
He's a boy called Jew. Gypsy. Stopthief. Runt. He's a boy who lives
in the streets of Warsaw. He's a boy who wants to be a Nazi some-
day, with tall, shiny jackboots of his own. Until the day that suddenly makes him change his mind—the day he realizes it's safest of
all to be nobody.

Memories of Summer • Ruth White • 978-0-440-22921-6
In 1955, thirteen-year-old Lyric describes her older sister Summer's
descent into mental illness, telling Summer's story with humor,
courage, and love.

35674052462927